The Elder Terror

Steven Duggan

**Oyster
Books**

ISBN: 9781981010837

Do not go gentle into that good night.
Old age should burn and rave at close of day.

[Dylan Thomas]

It's better to burn out than to fade away.
My, my. Hey, hey.

[Neil Young]

ONE

I was in Dublin City the afternoon of the first death. I was returning to collect the last of my belongings from an apartment off Dawson Street where I lived for a period shortly after I separated from my wife. I intended to park my car in the multi-storey on Schoolhouse Lane: turning into Molesworth Street, however, I was immediately aware of a commotion. Traffic was halted in both directions and there were three garda cars parked across the gates of the Dail, the guards directing drivers to turn about and go back the way they'd come. One of the garda cars was parked at an angle which suggested it had come down Kildare Street the wrong way. A knot of people was gathering on the pavement in front of Buswell's Hotel, straining to see past the cordon to what lay beyond. As I sat in my car I was passed by two women walking away from the scene, one holding the other tight against her shoulder and both clearly distressed. My first thought was that a cyclist had gone beneath the wheels of a car. Given how cyclists were treated in the city centre – and the ridiculous risks which some of them took – such an event was not uncommon.

I was stuck in a line some three or four cars back from the junction, and didn't have the space to turn about as some of those behind me were doing. I heard sirens approaching from Nassau Street and a fire engine appeared, pulling to a halt with a loud keening of its air brakes, further blocking my view. Reasoning that I was stuck there for the duration, I turned off my engine and stepped out of the car. Word was traveling back about some terrible accident in front of the Dail, a good number of those present busily relaying this news via their mobile phones.

This was Mary Connolly.

If you have forgotten the details, Mary was a seventy-one-year-old woman from Beara in County Galway who had travelled to Dublin by train earlier that morning. She walked the mile and a half from Huston Station to the Dail, stood before the gates and took a short-barrelled shotgun from a Tesco Eco-Save bag, turning it upon herself and pulling both triggers with what witnesses described as a practiced ease quite at odds with her frail appearance. Both chambers were filled with shot and the force of the blast removed most of Mary's head and upper torso, spraying the pavement and the forecourt of the parliament building with a cloud of pink and grey detritus. Press reports described how the silhouette of the railings could be seen upon the paving inside the gates, grey stripes running upward through the blood splatter.

Mary was a mother of four and a grandmother of nine. She had run her own solicitor's practice in Tuam prior to her retirement and continued to offer free legal advice to neighbours in the small community where she lived a full and what appeared to be a happy life, prior to that Thursday afternoon.

Her suicide dominated newspaper and television coverage in the lead up to Christmas. She left no note behind to explain her extraordinary actions and theories about her motives ran from dementia to some undetermined political protest about everything from health cuts, to the water charge. For almost a fortnight, it remained a subject of gossip and speculation in coffee shops and around festive dinner tables the length of the country.

Until the others.

Until Mark Noble on December 29th.

Until Thomas Quinn on New Year's Day, as the last bell rang out across Cork City.

Until Joan and Andrew Cuddy and then, later the same week, Pat and Eileen Fleming, in Wexford and Dublin respectively.

Until it became clear that these were not random acts but chapters in a horror story which had only begun to unfold. A story - although I was unaware of this at that time - which my own mother had helped to set in motion.

TWO

I should say something of my circumstances here and explain how I came to share my mother's house during the height of the terror. It was a little over ten months since my wife of seven years had invited me to pursue a life elsewhere, on the grounds that I had barely been with her in the first place. She provided me with a litany of proofs of my absence from our marriage while arranging the three suitcases into which she had gathered my belongings in our hallway. She had called a taxi immediately she spied me walking up the drive from the evening train. It wasn't until it drove away with my suitcases in the trunk that I appreciated the shrewdness of her actions, in effectively ensuring that both the house and our family car had transitioned to her ownership. But my ignorance of her intelligence had featured large in the litany of my faults she had enumerated, even as the taxi driver heaved my cases into the boot.

My crime, such as it was, came down to this: I had taken her for granted. The added charges – that I was incapable of seeing the good in anything or anyone, that my conversation was nothing but a tirade of complaints about the meanest and most inconsequential of things, that I finished her every sentence, constantly overruled her in public and regarded affection as something that was owed, rather than earned, were but further echoes of this theme. (There were some other charges laid against my character, but to be honest I wasn't really listening.) In short, I had been a lousy husband. A view my mother did nothing to contradict when I moved in with her in our old family home immediately before Christmas, having proven as poor as housemate as I had a spouse over the course of the six short weeks I spent in a work colleague's apartment on Dawson Street.

"Everything Laura said to you was true, Dominic", she told me as we sat down to tea together that first evening. "You were as useless a husband as you were a child. Your father and I despaired of your ever seeing beyond your own nose to recognise the existence, let alone the needs, of other people. You were quite capable of standing in the midst of a fire you had lit yourself whilst waiting for others to rescue you, and this is not going to be another of those occasions." She had followed this up with a list of strict does and don't, the contravening of any of which would result in my immediate expulsion from the house. To be honest, I had been rather surprised when she agreed to take me back in in the first place. Perhaps it had been the Christmas spirit; though God knows there had never been much of that in evidence in that house. Or the bad light it might have placed her in with her friends, had she refused to do so at that particular time of year? Whatever the cause, I was grateful, and agreed to every one of the conditions she set without protest. It was well over a month before I discovered the real reason she had allowed me to move home.

My mother was a fiercely independent woman. Ever since my father died at forty-nine, when I was a little over nine years of age and she was still a relatively young woman of thirty-three, she had been required to fashion a life for the pair of us without any of the support one might naturally expect to follow upon the loss of a spouse. My father – evidently as hapless and selfish a husband as I – was long estranged from his own parents on foot of some distant betrayal, the details of which were never explained to me. He had married my mother late, when he was in his late thirties and she was a full decade younger. Whatever first flush of romantic feeling might have led to that union had passed by the time of my earliest recollections. In truth, my recollections are likely in part a construction based on my mother's recounting of the various details of my childhood. I was too young, and he too absent a father, for me to retain more than a few disconnected memories of our time together.

I do remember him standing on the side-lines watching me play rugby at the age of five or six. Don't get me wrong: I was never proficient in any sport. I had gone along on his insistence, one of the many children whose fathers hoped against hope that their offspring would demonstrate a facility they themselves had lacked in their own youths, as if to put a lie to the memory. I no doubt spent the afternoon pursuing the others about the field at a distance respectful of my safety, or dropping the oval should it have the misfortune to end up in my hands. As cowardly as I might have been, I had an inflated sense of honour with respect to the safety of my friends; the red mist descending upon me in such instances as I am told it did whenever I was denied some treat or privilege by my parents. Thus it was that when my current best friend (these seemed to change at regular intervals, separated by lengthy periods of solitude) was felled by a straight-arm tackle well after the ball had gone, I ran at the offending player and kicked him as hard as I could upon the shin. Thankfully the referee intervened before his teammates exacted justice, expelling me from the field amid a chorus of boos and threats of violent repercussion from the thin line of supporters along the touchline. Some parents included, I seem to remember. My father, however, was virtually glowing with pride, his whole face altered by what I recognised must have been a grin. He placed his arm about my shoulder as he walked me back to the car, saying nothing of course. But that moment, as he marched me off in disgrace to the catcalls of a goodly number of our neighbours, has lodged in my memory like a teenage kiss.

In the main, however, my memories of him are restricted to that part of his body not obscured by the leaves of a book or the sheets of a newspaper, a distant grunt coming from the far side of his locus of interest every time I tried to engage his attention with some childish matter. As he was stationary, my mother was a constant blur of activity, ever bustling and fussing about us both in pursuit of household tasks or her apparently endless succession of 'interests', from weaving to gardening, from water colouring to calligraphy and her numerous involvements with community groups including help the aged (irony of ironies!) and the Vincent de Paul. In support of these pursuits, she read everything. Books grew in ungainly piles about the kitchen and dining room, and I even spied a tower of them beside the bed on her side, on one of the rare occasions I stole into their bedroom. They never seemed to find a place upon our bookshelves, which were rigorously protected by my father and arrayed so as to advertise his intellect to any visitor. Her instruction manuals and research works were not regarded by him as 'proper' books. Even after he died, his neatly catalogued shelves remained untouched and I remember how disappointed I was, years later, when I discovered that rather than the canon of European literature they seemed largely made up of thrillers by Alexander McClean and Hammond Innes, and books about the two World Wars.

As a Church of Ireland family, we were outside of the mainstream in any case. At that time, COI families comprised less than two percent of the Irish population, and although the town where we lived was virtually unique on the island in having a protestant community close to a quarter of the total number of denizens, this number was made up of those from a variety of churches, Presbyterian, Methodist and others, who banded together in an almost incestuous clan, forever gathering for fetes and festivals, or remained in virtual seclusion. My father tended toward the latter, an isolation alleviated only by regular visit to one of his favoured hostelries, and my mother to the former, so that they seemed always to be in different places, whichever parent being 'in' that evening de facto entrusted with my care. Whoever this might be left me to my own devices, reading or patiently fending off my constant enquiries until I eventually tired of the effort to engage them. I was a solitary child, all in all, and adopted the habit of reading in much the way other children followed their parents into crime, or alcoholism. It is little wonder, I suppose, that I would prove such a distant and useless husband. Though I found my mother's criticism of my failings in this respect a little harsh, given that she clearly believed there had been no contribution on her part to my shortcomings.

If I had been a poor husband, and a disappointment as a child, I would prove an even greater failure as a carer. For it became clear to me within a month that my mother's decision to readmit me to the family home - and to tolerate me once there – was directly linked to her own failing health. The ironies could not have been invisible to her. A woman known for her independence and strength, who had devoted many evenings and weekends over the years to efforts to support the elderly and infirm of our parish, was now slowly but surely joining their ranks. As hapless a lump as I may have been, I was her best hope of maintaining her privacy and independence in the years to come and of staving off the horrific spectre of being forced to quit her home for a place in some residential facility. Once this became clear to me, I admit that I exploited it to a degree. Knowing I was no longer there on sufferance, and that an infraction of the rules was unlikely to result in my immediate exile, I began to settle back into my old ways. It has often been remarked to me by colleagues from larger families than ours that they found themselves reverting to their old selves immediately upon returning to their family home, for Christmas or other such occasion. Old rivalries and rituals recommenced as if they had but recently left home, the personas they had abandoned long before revived immediately they stepped through the front door. So it was for me. Apart from a token effort to do my own laundry – a task which I was quickly excused – I picked up effectively where I had left off some twenty years before, coming home from work each evening in expectation of a dinner upon the table and reading for hours in my father's old armchair before retiring to bed. I will even confess to working my way through several of his volumes, finding them much more entertaining, and racier, than I had imagined. My mother bustled about me, occasionally giving out about one of my many lapses (I affected not to hear these) and voraciously consuming both the printed and television news. She also took to writing a journal at the kitchen table, and it is only recently that I realised this must have marked the commencement of what would become her 'Manifesto'.

Thankfully, she was still financially independent. My father's job as a senior civil servant meant that he had decent life insurance when he passed and she had also received an inheritance from an uncle who died the very same month, as fate would have it. She missed her uncle very much, I believe. She had been, in the parlance of the time, "well left". The family home was paid off, and her various pensions and investments provided her with a comfortable living and, more importantly, the ability to maintain her independence. Several of her friends had already been forced to abandon their homes and take refuge in their children's houses, regaling her with stories of simmering disputes with daughters and sons-in-law, living as non-paying guests and constantly under obligation. Others – as a result of illness or misfortune – had had to resort to residential care of some sort. This prospect filled her with terror. She had turned seventy a few months before I returned, and watched her own health and mental acuity with a gimlet eye, ever on the lookout for any sign of mental wastage. I think this was the first impetus for her keeping a journal. As crosswords were viewed by her contemporaries as a vaccine against Alzheimer's, journaling may have offered her both intellectual exercise and an opportunity to capture her views in the absence of some other audience. I of course was singularly unfit to play such a role. As I have stated, I was never her confidant. She viewed me, if not without a mother's tolerance, as a useless lump. My fetching up on her doorstep after a failed marriage could not have done much to mitigate such a view. And in truth I was happy enough to adopt this persona, idleness and unreliability bringing with it the freedom to avoid responsibility of any kind.

What started as a diversion changed at some point, and by April I increasingly found myself the first to go up to bed, my mother still bent over her Moleskin journal with her Mont Blanc spewing forth line after line in her elegant script. She barely seemed to notice me at such times, and if her departure from a rigorously maintained schedule struck me as unusual, it was of little concern to me. Breakfast continued to be served the following morning before I departed for the train, and everything else continued as normal. I have discovered myself, in the course of composing this memoir, how writing benefits from your dedicating a particular time to its pursuit, in line with one's personal timetable. For me the early hours are best, before the world awakens. The first drafts of this account were all written before eight each morning, having risen at six-thirty and taken the dog for a walk. Nelson – our elderly lab – has grown increasingly disinclined to join me on my morning constitutional, and I suspect he may shortly follow his mistress from the house. Had she been a more sentimental woman I might well have investigated the possibility of the dog being buried alongside her: though I believe there are prohibitions against such practices.

My mother found the late hours more conducive to writing, settling at the kitchen table with a pot of jasmine tea beside her, occasionally supplemented by a small plate of biscuits. Lincoln Creams were her particular favourite, and I still find myself pausing before the biscuit shelf in Donnybrook Fair, despite the fact that I have never cared for their slightly aniseed flavour. I don't believe she ever stayed up much past midnight – at least, not until later events made such a practice necessary, as the volume of her correspondence grew.

How our letterbox came to act as a chute for a voluminous pile of letters from points far and near (not to mention the endless stream of emails and social media messages which accompanied this) is, of course, the subject of this memoir. How did an elderly protestant woman from a well-heeled suburb of a small city became a global figure, reshaping public perceptions in such a profound and tragic fashion? As is always the case, I suspect, it was the power of words. Whether these are the words of the authors themselves, or journalistic accounts of their actions or pronouncements, only words have the ability to shift the world upon its axis. My mother believed that those who read neither books nor the quality newspapers were effectively non-citizens, excluded from the process of living: 'the unconsidered life', etc. She was never a snob, my mother, but believed herself justified in regarding those without an interest in matters of the world – whatever their social standing – as collectively devalued. An interest in the tabloid press or celebrity 'culture' would earn them her active disdain.

It began with a letter to The Irish Times. That first missive, with its formative declarations about the role and the treatment of the elderly, has become a key document in the history of subsequent events. It needs to be stressed yet again that there is no call to action in that communication. I believe the thought that her letter would in any way serve to bring about the horrors which were to follow would have immediately dissuaded her from submitting it. It was, nonetheless, a rallying cry. The advent of social media and electronic forms of news may perhaps have skewed the readership of the paper of record towards her natural audience, but the impact of her letter could not have been predicted. The volume of responses proved so great in the coming week that the newspaper dedicated a feature to what it called 'the voice of the aged' as a new constituency in Irish politics.

There is nothing inflammatory – or indeed original – in the substance of that letter. It was but another of those outraged epistles which accompanied the scandal regarding the abuse of elders at nursing homes in Carlow and West Dublin. My mother's vanity is still apparent to me in her positioning of herself as an advocate for, rather than of that community. It is only in its closing sentence that it differed from those more mannered expressions of shock and concern, with its call to others wishing to become involved in "an active protest" to join an online community whose aim would be to represent the interests of these most marginalised of people.

I'm not sure what shocked me most: finding my mother's name amongst the authors of that day's letters to the editor, as I read the paper on the train that morning - or the thought that my mother knew how to establish "an online community". It subsequently transpired that she had taken an evening class in the nearby secondary school as part of a program aimed at facilitating an exchange between transition year students and those for whom the digital revolution had passed largely unnoticed. I cannot imagine that she would have been an easy student for whichever sixteen-year-old was tasked with teaching her the rudiments of the internet and social media.

I conducted a Google search of her name once I arrived at the office, and soon located her web page. It was in point of fact a free page for a service called petition.org which, according to the banner at the top of each page, allowed anyone to create and share a petition or fundraising page, most of these apparently devoted to the sponsorship of charity walks, marathons or mountain ascents.

"If you have been affected by the recent disclosures of elder abuse in the St Mitchen's and Rathmor nursing homes and wish to register your concern that such despicable acts have yet to become the subject of an independent inquiry, please sign our petition below." This short introduction was followed by a form to which people were encouraged to add their names, email addresses and locations, proceeded by a voting button. At the very base of the page was a counter to indicate how many people had already signed the petition. When I first visited, that number stood at 112. I remember the number, as it coincided with my father's birth date, December 1st. I left the page open on my desktop, and found myself compulsively returning to it over the course of the day to check how many additional petitioners had joined the cause. By the time I turned off my PC and headed for the train, that number had grown to over two thousand.

People of my age are still startled by the ability of social media to translate online presence into virtual word of mouth, and the speed at which this most expeditious form of Chinese whispers can spread. Somehow, by the time I arrived home and ate my evening meal, this number had grown to over thirty thousand. Subsequent investigations identified the majority of the signatories as coming from outside these waters, and the demographic was skewed toward a populace much younger than my mother, or the victims themselves. Facebook links had led in turn to Twitter entries, with one of these being picked up by a well-known rock star with a social conscience and an online following in the hundreds of thousands, who posted links to both the Irish Times account of the despicable treatment doled out to the residents of the care homes, and my mother's online petition. His 'tweet' in its turn was repeated by several of his celebrity followers and by socially-active individuals subscribing to one or more of these accounts, and by early the following day her petition stood at close to a quarter of a million signatories!

It was this which prompted a call from the journalist Eileen Hoy, who had tracked down my mother's phone number via Eircom's online directory (my mother did not have a mobile phone at this juncture). Perhaps the paper wished to highlight its own part in championing the issue, given that its letters page had promoted such an outpouring of ire and disgust (comments on the internet being much less restrained - and literate - than in the pages of the Paper Of Record) but whatever the intent, the result would be to elevate my mother from concerned citizen, to public figure. The article itself, and the manner in which the journalist used my mother's still quite temperate utterances to fashion a sensationalist piece, proved instructive to her, I suspect. I believe she recognised that the only way to gain or maintain interest in a cause of this nature was to embrace the feverish tone of the zealot. She had already become quite disillusioned at the speed with which the issue had vanished from the front pages, replaced by speculation about the upcoming budget and a report detailing a betting scandal in professional football.

Her petition, however, continued to build momentum. The feature article in The Irish Times (Online Advocate Draws International Attention to Care Home Abuses) was circulated in turn by those whose interest was still excited by the issue, and the call from Eileen Hoy was soon followed by an invitation to take part in the Dan Crowley talk show, which aired each afternoon during the rush-hour commute.

As poised and confident as my mother may have been in print, or amongst her peers, an appearance on national radio filled her with dread. For the first time, she shared these concerns with me. I had studiously avoided any mention of her petition or the newspaper article, taking her unwillingness to discuss it with me as an indication that she would not welcome my input. However, she now disclosed the fact that she was extremely nervous and went as far as to ask me whether I would drive her to the station on the appointed afternoon – the day immediately following the call from the station – so that she could compose herself in advance of the broadcast.

Her composure would soon desert her. I believe that she was entirely unprepared for the confrontational nature of such a medium. Rather than a gentle prompting of his subjects, Crowley's style was to deliberately provoke his guests (evasive politicians in the main) casting doubt upon both their views and the sincerity of their positions. This would normally prove quite effective, having the effect of provoking them into an impassioned defence.

But he did not know my mother. Having provided a brief precis of the issue for his listeners and introduced my mother as "the online activist May Burke", he immediately went on the attack, asking her whether she had seen the scandal as an opportunity to raise her own profile. Effectively accusing her of "hopping on the bandwagon" of elder abuse for personal gain! This had proved an excellent stratagem in the past. People unused to appearing on television or radio tend to be halting and unconvincing in the glare of a camera or when speaking into a microphone. Ruffling their feathers was often the best way to ensure they overcame their nervousness and spoke up, as it were. In my mother's case, the result was dramatic. Questioning my mother's integrity did not lead her to mount a passionate defence of her position, but to launch an outright assault upon Crowley himself.

"How dare you!" she began, going on to describe him as a "parasite" who preyed upon the victims of genuine tragedies in order to boost his rating. She went on to accuse the media in general of ignoring what she described as "the single largest issue of the day" and of effectively acting as accomplices of those who had visited "unimaginable horrors" upon the most helpless members of our society. It was here that she first drew the comparison between young children and the elderly. How was it, she asked, that the abuse of a single child could occasion a detailed examination of the nation's soul, whereas the "violent assault" upon equally helpless people "tucked away, out of sight" in old folks' homes could be ignored, despite offering at least as unflattering a view into the temperament of the nation? Inviting the shell-shocked Crowley to imagine his own future in such an institution, "abandoned by your children and by a society you helped to create and loyally served for decades, and which you paid to establish with your taxes", she painted a vivid portrait of the presenter as a lonely, infirm and helpless old man, treated as an inconvenient burden upon that same society and proceeding toward a rapid demise - bullied and mistreated by those entrusted with his care, too afraid to speak out even if capable of doing so, and viewed on the one hand as a financial encumbrance and on the other as a source of profit. Said profit margins best augmented by hiring the least qualified and most poorly paid of carers, and returns maximized by serving substandard food in conditions best described as subhuman. Referring to the care homes in St Mitchen's and Rathmor as "Gulags" she concluded by calling Crowley an "unconscionable little shit", throwing her headphones at him, and storming out of the studio.

As you might imagine, this provoked something of a reaction. Crowley's rivals were quick to seize upon his misfortune, gleefully detailing the way in which he had been "humiliated by a pensioner" and solemnly declaring their own bona fides. It helped that Crowley was a divisive figure. For every listener who viewed him as a controversial but provocative commentator, a provocateur if you like, there were three who thought him an obnoxious windbag and self-publicist. The tabloids went to town. "'Take That You Little Sh*t!" was the headline in The Sun. The Herald went with the more restrained "How Dare You, Crowley!" whilst The Irish Times ran a follow-up by Eileen Hoy describing how "former Irish Times correspondent May Burke" had "upbraided" the talk show host for "making light of the plight of senior citizens". My mother's anger and embarrassment – I can still remember the tension of that silent journey home – was soon replaced by something else. As sensationalist as the coverage might have been, it also served to return the issue of the treatment of the elderly to the front pages. In this, she learnt a valuable lesson. As uncomfortable as she might have been with the role of "firebrand", she also recognised that such an approach was perhaps the most effective course to adopt in pursuit of her agenda. I should stress that at this point that 'agenda' extended no further than the raising of public consciousness.

The most common comparison made in the course of those few days was with Bob Geldorf's outburst during the broadcast for Live Aid, when the rock star smashed a coffee table in anger at the way in which the event he had organized to draw attention to starving people was descending into a variety show for the entertainment of its viewers. Just as that outpouring of anger served to bring people's attention back to the matter at hand, my mother determined to use her own fervour as a vehicle to keep public attention focused upon the care of the elderly. Geldof himself did an interview, hailing my mother as a hero for a forgotten generation, and he was soon joined by a host of celebrity fans, including the broadcaster Stephen Fry and the popular boy-band One Direction, who gave a moving interview on BBC Television about the ways in which their own grandmothers had shaped their lives, calling upon their young fans to "reach out" to elderly relatives and seniors within their communities to remind them that they were "not forgotten". News of my mother's campaign soon reached beyond these shores, and her petition by this point had over one-point-five-million signatories. One fanciful journalist stated that this meant that she had more supporters "than the entire government front bench" and raised the prospect of her standing as an independent candidate for Irish President at the conclusion of the current incumbent's term in office.

I have spent considerable time trying to identify the point at which things changed so radically and so portentously from an effort to increase public awareness, to a revolution. I believe such a description is justified. If those who occupied the General Post Office in 1916 can be hailed as revolutionaries, in that their words and actions served to reshape a nation, can the same not be said of those who joined my mother's crusade? Measured purely in terms of the number who died, it is arguably more deserving of that name.

I am concerned – as are many others who have written of this period – that Ireland's community of older citizens are not portrayed as hapless recruits to someone else's cause. They had considerably more agency than such a shallow reading of events would suggest. Yes, my mother's campaign may have provided the impetus for their uprising – and her manifesto was regularly cited as their 'proclamation of independence' – but the decision to escalate matters was, and should rightly be regarded as, theirs.

The first sign of this growing activism came on her website. Whereas before she had used her WordPress page to post her own views, and sparingly at that, over the following week it became a message board for people of all ages, hosting comments and calls to action. It soon became impossible for my mother to respond to all of these, but this didn't seem to matter. A whole online conversation was now developing between these people themselves, with new, more elaborate websites popping up daily, some dedicated to my mother and citing extracts from her interviews like truisms from Gandhi or Einstein, most of them acting as feeder sites for her petition... and using a language and a tone utterly at odds with her own reasoned and measured approach. Some commentators, somewhat cynically, have suggested that these had been set up primarily to benefit from the 'traffic' which any mention of my mother generated and the advertising revenue which accompanied it. There were rants from YouTubers, 'memes' which substituted images of my mother for those of movie stars, accompanied by lines of dialogue from their films (one with a quote from the Liam Neeson movie 'Taken' went viral in the week following her interview) and all of it serving to transform the public perception of her from upper-middle-class widow, to some kind of vengeful revolutionary.

Did this turn her head? I'm not sure. The most charitable view is that she exploited it to keep public attention focused on the rights and treatment of the elderly (the term still being in common parlance at the time). The strength of feeling these sites generated and encouraged however could not fail to have influenced her. Perhaps even to radicalise her. My own belief, having witnessed first-hand how she was overwhelmed by the constant twenty-four-hour barrage of requests and misquotes, sleeping less and operating in a perpetual maelstrom of emotions from anger to incomprehension – is that she took up her pen in an attempt to control it. To step in, and attempt to place some parameters upon this rapidly growing movement. Her Manifesto, I would suggest, was an attempt to bring all of this to a close. A seventy-year-old woman, trying to put her arms around the internet! And doing so in a state of exhaustion, her judgement affected by the cacophony of voices surrounding her calling out for direction.

Postscript: December 2017

I am often asked what lay behind my mother's transformation from concerned citizen to outraged zealot; or firebrand, as she has also been called. The person who penned a letter to the Irish Times inviting people to register their support by signing an online petition is not the same person, it is argued, as the woman who assaulted journalists and helmed large public gatherings demanding action from authorities at the highest level. For me – seeing her passion grow on a daily basis – that change appeared more incremental than sudden. There may however have been some specific catalysts in that progression, and I believe I have identified one of these.

Several months after penning this memoir I came upon a letter from a resident of a care home, buried within the voluminous pile of her correspondence. It is an account of life in one of these institutions, penned not by one of those who resorted to extreme means to draw attention to their plight, but by someone beaten down to a point at which any further resistance appeared futile. Someone with every reason to end his life, that is, but deprived of the will to do so. It makes for difficult reading so I shall suffice by providing you with an extract, taking due care to excise names and location.

"His name is John _____. I have no idea why he has decided to persecute me. There is nothing I have done – nothing I do – to explain his hatred for me. I was neither rich nor important before I arrived here. Just a normal man. No better – I have repeatedly told him – than him. But it doesn't seem to matter. He persecutes me anyway. He hates me anyway. Whatever I do - whatever I say - he makes it clear that nothing will change. That every day he will do all in his power to make my life not just miserable but a living hell.

I am almost past caring now. Past praying. Past despair. If I cry out no one will hear me. No one will step in for me. No one will care. And what should I say anyway? How could I prove any of it? My daughter calls to see me and he stands down the corridor and stares at me over her shoulder. Out of sight of her but threatening me. Making it clear what he will do to me – to her! – if I as much as whisper a word against him. I am his prisoner. I am his slave. He has made me nothing.

She'll go and he'll start again. The old things. Or maybe something new. He tells me he likes to try new things. I won't know when. That is another of his things. I'll be looking away. Or asleep. Or in the bathroom - they all have keys. Like the first time he pissed on me. Stood there and pissed, while I was sat. Covering my knees and my legs. Wetting my trousers where they were down. Making fun of me when I came out saying that I'd wet myself. Laughing. And when he stood beside my bed with his prick out. Playing with it as he leaned over me. And smiling. So that was what I saw when I woke up. Right by my face.

He likes to hurt me too. Hides it though - he's so good at that. He reaches round me like he's helping me eat and digs his nails into my shoulder. Pushes them into my skin. Hits me in the back of my head as he passes. Stands on my feet. Sticks his fingers and almost his whole hand into my mouth. Always out of sight. No one sees. If anyone does – if it's one of us – they pretend not to. Rather me than them.

The door is open you see Mrs Burke. I could walk out. But I don't have bus fare. Can't talk properly now. Can't stand how people look at me. And I'm too weak now to run. He doesn't let me sleep. I pray for when he is not there but have to wait then. The waiting is as bad.

The worst is when he baths me."

The letter is not dated. I can only hope that the old man (or woman, for it is unclear from the letter which) has escaped their ordeal now. I am confident the letter arrived some short while before her radio appearance, judging by the letters to either side of it. To read them, you would think *all* 'old folks' homes' as they called them were Gulags. But for me, this one was the worst of all the letters she received. If anyone wants to know what 'radicalised' her then I would invite them to take a look at this pile of missals.

THREE

I will not transcribe each article of my mother's Manifesto here. The document is well-known, and easily accessible online. Certain passages however bear repeating. Those for which I can provide some elucidation, or background. I did not, as some have suggested, contribute, co-author or edit so much as a word of it. It was much later that she began to include me, and only then because the constant attentions of the press had made her a virtual prisoner in her own home, leaving her with nobody else in whom to confide. The notion that I incited her in any way is equally preposterous. My mother may have spoken to me of her views, but she never gave my opinions the slightest consideration. I may perhaps have been guilty of failing to try to temper her views; but being in her confidence was an experience for which I was unprepared and - loathsome as this might sound - I did not want to do anything which would banish me from it. The only 'co-authors' were those who took her words and used them to justify their own extraordinary acts of protest. I also want to stress that the *responsibility* for those deaths needs to be laid firmly at the feet of those who perpetuated the abuses she and her followers sought to remedy.

Where does evil originate, we wonder? In the torrid lives of the perpetrators of such acts? In the casual cruelties inflicted upon them in their own past by parents incapable of feeling or displaying love? In the lessons learned in their childhoods which in turn beget their own failings? In those acquired by their parents or grandparents, and so on even to Adam? I know that genetics plays unequal games, some of these weaknesses diluted or even eradicated over time and others amplified until they reach a state of perfect malice, accompanied by the capacity to visit it on others with or without conscience.

What should we make, then, of the evils to which the residents of St Mitchen's and Rathmor were subjected? Should we react with horror? With anger? With stoic understanding, or even pity? Our obligation in the face of evil is not to blame, but to take action. We may not understand such things, but we must do all that we can to stop them. My mother understood this. But as soon became clear in the wake of the publication of the reports detailing the care home abuses, the government did not. New edicts were issued and new standards of care published. But no genuine effort was made to invest in the rigorous monitoring system required to enforce these. This was evidence either of a lack of political will, or of a belief that this constituency lacked the widespread support or sufficiently strong a voice to affect the outcome of any subsequent election. Through their inertia they, too, are culpable. Had any real effort been made to protect the rights of those in the innumerable facilities about the country whose cruelties mirrored or surpassed those of St Mitchen's (where residents were force-fed, badgered, and left to slowly rot) then it is unlikely that Mary Connolly or those who followed her lead would have resorted to such desperate measures.

The simple truth is that their plight did not matter. The care of the elderly was still regarded as a cost - as an imposition upon the national purse. As my mother said, no heed was paid to the fact that these same people were "the creators of the society in which you live. The citizens who, via long years of service to the state at rates of taxation well in excess of those you complain of, paid for the benefits and rights which you enjoy, and they are denied."

I must admit that I still find the term 'Manifesto' somewhat grandiose. Her writings may have taken on a greater significance, but the fact remains that this was little more than a lengthy blog-post by a woman of advanced years. All she was trying to do, I think, was to wrest control of the dialogue from those with more extreme views. The cranks. The rabid and the incendiary. The (and pardon my language) gobdaws and the gobshites. In setting out her 'articles' she was merely trying to limit the forms of protest used by those who supported her petition. Looked at in this light they are little more than the general principles for nonviolent protest stolen wholesale from King and Gandhi.

Protests should be non-violent regardless of provocation - no one should be harmed, or have their safety endangered, as a result of your protest.

Protests should directly support the primary objective of this campaign - to draw attention to the shameful manner in which older members of our society are marginalised, mistreated and ignored.

All arguments should be directly relevant to our primary objective and communicated in a language appropriate for public use.

A simple enough set of strictures - and in no way a license for what was to follow.

Her blog went viral. I am told that it was (often poorly) translated into more than twenty languages in the course of one week. The anger she expressed in that fateful interview with the journalist Crowley is evident in every paragraph, and played no small part in its dissemination. This was a rallying cry to people who were already disaffected, and who had been silenced for too long. It is extraordinary in one way that technology would prove the vehicle for revolution, given the demographic. But I am assured that, far from proving luddites, elders in fact embraced social media early and wholeheartedly. It was often their best or only way of keeping contact with children and grandchildren, particularly when these had moved far from their orbit. For many, Skype and Facebook were the tools they used to keep in touch, and email their most common form of communication. Texting was also popular, if less so. The use of Twitter was much more skewed toward younger supporters, as were attendant technologies such as Vine and Instagram, which were to play such a pivotal role in ensuring this became a global, rather than a national protest.

All of these "engines of misinformation" as Taoiseach Kenny called them kicked into action in the aftermath of the deaths of the Cuddys and the Flemings.

We have forgotten the lack of response which followed the deaths of Mark Noble and Thomas Quinn. No one had yet connected the dots between these apparently unrelated events: in Thomas Quinn's case because his suicide note was not discovered until early in the New Year. We forget, too, the high rate of suicide which already existed amongst older people. At that time, it had already surpassed that of teenage suicides, and was probably considerably higher, given that coroners were loath to attribute cause of death to this, rather than as "an accidental overdose" or "accidental death" caused by a lapse in concentration or age-related infirmity. In this way, the majority of deaths by electrocution, single-person automobile fatality and a myriad forms of sudden death were routinely classified as "not suspicious" in the parlance. In those cases where suicide was the most likely cause of death, this finding was often obscured for the supposed benefit of surviving relatives. What interest could be served by adding to their distress, particularly given the likelihood that their remaining years would have been few and perhaps unhappy one in any case? If suicide truly is a cry for help, then those cries went unanswered.

Until the week of January 4th.

We remember the deaths of the Cuddys and the Flemings most clearly, perhaps, because these were joint suicides. Decisions a long-married and loving couple had taken and acted upon together. These were not the result of some "sudden black moment". In each case their actions had been premeditated and meticulously planned, and clearly not the actions of people who were mentally confused, or in despair. The very public nature of their deaths may be the reason why news of those events spread so quickly around the world: but they had also taken steps to ensure this would come to pass. The suicide notes they left behind were exemplars of clear and lucid prose (a skill sadly in abeyance amongst the younger generation) and immediately made accessible to the news media. In the Flemings' case, their grand gesture involved a level of preparation worthy of the most carefully planned 'bank job'.

Monday January 4th was a typical day for the time of year. True, there had been some unseasonably high winds, and localised flooding in the wake of storm Desmond still affected large swathes of the country. This had largely passed the capital city by, however. Traffic in Dublin city centre was heavy but moving, Grafton Street still a throng of shoppers and commuters making their way toward the LUAS

Station at Stephen's Green or the taxi ranks and bus stops. There were three horse-drawn carriages still stationed outside the Soldier's Gate when the Cuddys approached the foremost hackney to request a ride, despite it being an unpopular time for tourists. The hackney, a Patrick Fleming (no relation) said he considered turning them down, knowing the disruption his carriage could cause to the smooth flow of traffic in the vicinity. Mrs Cuddy had reasoned with him however that traffic was already at a virtual standstill, and his hansom was more likely to be given leeway to traverse from lane to lane than "some arrogant arse in a BMW", as she had put it. He relented, and they pulled out into the flow of traffic to begin a circumlocution of the green. He had refused their request to go on to Kildare Street and Merrion Square, begging the question as to whether their original intention had been to stage their protest at the same spot where Mary Connolly had shot herself a few weeks before. Mr Fleming could not recall their having any baggage when they mounted the trap, but close circuit images confirmed that they had hidden their weapons in their coats, which they had draped over their knees as a bulwark against the cold. They sat far apart on the raised seat behind the driver, holding hands across the space between them. They would remain conjoined in this fashion until Mr Cuddy lost consciousness, his wife slumping down into the footwell shortly afterward. There were no cameras with a clear view of the moment they caused their injuries, but two motorists testified that they had leaned across to kiss each other, holding the embrace for several seconds before burying their hands beneath their coats, resuming their previous positions with an arm draped over the carriage to either side. A post-mortem confirmed that rather than inflicting the fatal wounds to their own limbs, each had cut the other's wrist using identical blades which they then abandoned at their feet. The cuts were lateral rather than transverse, perhaps as an added insurance that they would not be prevented from their course of action by some amateur intervention. Despite this, it is almost certainly the case that their lives could have been saved had anyone with medical training been alerted to what was happening within the first couple of minutes. It later transpired that they had read extensively on the issue, and the incisions they made were sufficient to ensure that the trail of blood proceeded along the sides of the gleaming white carriage and onto the roadway, but not so deep as to cause the blood to spurt upwards, horrid as that description might be, which no doubt played a part in the length of time it took for people to become aware of the atrocity. The wounds they had made ensured a steady if staccato stream, two parallel lines of red as regularly spaced as cart tracks, until loss of blood pressure halted the flow in the final moments of exsanguination.

The horror and chaos which followed has been well documented. Even today, it seems almost inconceivable that two elderly people would choose to end their lives in this way, politely holding hands in a form of conveyance more suited to a courting couple in the farthest reaches of our history, while their life's blood tumbled in its wake. At five-thirty pm – less than a half hour later, and in time for the six o'clock national news broadcast – the email they had composed the previous day was delivered to all of the major news outlets, having been scheduled for a delayed posting using some commonly available software. Its contents were not disclosed at that time, nor in the evening news broadcast, while Gardaí worked to inform the next of kin. The following day's newspapers however shared the full text, some displaying a facsimile of the 'letter' on their front page.

People have asked why my mother did not speak out then. Why she didn't issue some statement, or conduct an interview in the press to call for a halt to such extreme forms of protest. In truth, I am not sure. Part of me thinks she was simply too shocked, too overwhelmed by the manner in which things had snowballed and appeared to have taken on an independent life and momentum. She may have believed that her voice would no longer carry any weight. There is no doubt in my mind that the reaction on social media – on her own pages and others – played some part. Here - in particular amongst the Cuddys' peers - there was no clamour for reason or moderation. Quite the contrary. Instead, the mood alternated between anger and triumph. "Now they'll listen to us!" was the prevailing sentiment.

And of course, they didn't.

"It is not despair or hopelessness which led us to end our lives. We are neither of us mentally ill, nor suffering from an incurable disease. To ensure such speculation would not proliferate we subjected ourselves to exhaustive medical checks on January 2nd of this year, the results of which are attached. For confirmation, please contact Dr Indira Balakrishnan at Wexford General Hospital. At the time of writing, we are both of sound mind and body. Further, in case it is suggested that we acted under duress or at another's direction, we wish to stress that this was a decision taken privately and independently. We are aware of the distress the nature of our deaths will have caused to our family and friends, and extend our sincere apologies to them, all of whom we have loved ardently and to the very end. We have had wonderful lives, which you have helped to shape and have filled with so many moments of joy. We also wish to apologise to anybody who may have had to witness our final moments and for the distress this may have caused. It was not our intention to shock, or to upset you. Our intention was to shock and upset our entire nation.

For too long, those of us of advanced years have been an ignored minority in our country. Invisible not just to those who set the political agenda – who vote for reductions in pensions, or to curtail the provision of health care for elders and others in greatest need – but to the very communities in which they live. We pass amongst you unnoticed, occasionally registering as an annoyance when we take too long to board a bus or train, or require extra time at a serving counter. The world in which you live, as May Burke put it in her recent press interview, is the world we created. Yet far from receiving your gratitude, or even the simple recognition that years of toil and effort in the formative years of our society would surely demand, we are treated as a burden.

Voiceless. Powerless. Even superfluous. We felt it was high time to cry "Enough!"

And there you have it. By referencing my mother directly in their final communique, the Cuddys ensured that once again she was thrust into the position of acting as spokesperson for an entire generation.

Even this might have passed, had the Flemings not chosen to treat the Cuddys deaths as both an example - and a challenge. For it is clear from their correspondence that they deliberately sought not only to reinforce the message of their predecessors, but to outdo them in execution. The word execution, I have just realised, is somewhat ironic, given that the place they chose for their public suicide was a building directly linked to the execution of a group of men later viewed as the fathers of our nation. Did they, too, see themselves as martyrs? I suspect so. And their choice of venue was no doubt intended to suggest this.

It still seems extraordinary to me that a functioning post office – indeed, the largest such in Dublin City and environs – should have such lax security that an elderly couple could gain easy egress to the roof of the building. It later transpired that they had researched this in detail beforehand, paying several visits to the GPO before January 12th in order to determine the level of attention paid to visitors, and using web searches to obtain detailed floorplans of the building. Such details were freely available online, given that the essential structure of the building was unchanged in the years since 1916.

Unlike the Cuddys, who had harnessed the power of the press in the aftermath of their grand gesture, the Flemings – Patrick (Pat) aged seventy-one and his wife Eileen, sixty-eight, both former schoolteachers and active union members in their day – sought to attract attention from the first. Having successfully barred the doors to the stairwells on either side, to prevent anyone from following them onto the roof, Eileen took out her mobile phone and rang the news office of The Irish Independent. As a further guarantee of attention, she used her phone to post comments on the reader sections of the Sky News and RTE News websites. Sky News in fact offered her several ways in which to draw attention to this 'emerging news story', including email and a dedicated text number to which members of the public could send "texts, pictures and videos". There was quite a high wind swirling about the top of the building, making it difficult for the journalist who received her call to make out the details of her message, so it was fortunate from their point of view that Eileen availed of the opportunity to follow up her call with a text detailing what they intended to do and the exact hour, accompanied by a short video taken from the roof using her phone, so as to establish the veracity of the call. It might have seemed slightly unpatriotic to have utilized the services of a British news service, but her choice proved wise. While RTE and the Indo were still scrambling to determine the truth of the messages they'd received, Sky News had already dispatched a television crew to O'Connell Street and alerted the guards to evacuate the area, once they'd taken up a position from which to film events.

As horrific as the Cuddys' final gesture had been - literally making the capital run red with blood - nothing could have prepared people for the spectacle of two pensioners throwing themselves off the roof of its most iconic building. Right up to the last minute, it appeared that they may be prevented from doing so. The fire brigade had begun to deploy a series of inflatable mats in front of the portico, reasoning that the Flemings would choose the apex of the building from which to leap. But the Flemings had prepared for this, instead taking up positions on either side of the acroteria; Pat taking a position on the left, at the feet of the winged Mercury (a deliberate irony) while

Eileen stood upon the plinth of Fidelity on the right, as a gesture perhaps to the bond which they had maintained throughout their fifty-year marriage. We are still unsure of the method they used to ensure their simultaneous descent, but no one who witnessed the scene, whether they were present amongst the vast which quickly gathered, or who watched any of the eyewitness videos which immediately promulgated upon the internet, despite the embargo imposed upon the television news channels, will ever forget the terrible majesty of their final moments as they plunged in concert, heads downward and arms tucked close to their sides like the champion Irish dancers they had been in their youth, toward their final resting place upon the paved walkway below.

There was method, it transpired, in the poses they adopted. As schoolteachers, they knew that a fall from a height of some fifty feet would be unlikely to kill them - and worse, might confine them to wheelchairs or otherwise incapacitate them for the remainder of their lives. By ensuring that they met the ground head-first, they had calculated that their deaths would be certain, and instantaneous.

The three stages of a public response to terror are concern, fear, and panic. It was at this point that the nation moved from the first to the second. Outright panic would be less than a fortnight away.

To understand her own reaction, it is necessary to understand something of my mother's character. She was, as I have stated, a fiercely independent woman. She may have been spared the financial burden of being a single mother - still something of a rarity in those times, when young girls who gave birth out of wedlock were often sent away and their offspring put up for adoption, or subject to worse fates as the scandalous history of the Magdalen laundries has well documented and when the expectation of young widows was that they would remarry following an appropriate period of mourning - but in all other respects she was called upon to display a fortitude quite beyond the norm for those of her sex following my father's death. Women at that time were still dependent upon their husbands to an extent we perhaps do not fully comprehend. A woman was required by law to quit her career upon marrying, and an unmarried woman of above twenty-five years of age was regarded as a 'spinster'. The nunneries were filled with women who had chosen a cloistered life in preference to becoming an indentured servant to the men of their household, a fate which awaited them should they fail in their efforts to find a husband. The decline in the numbers pursuing a religious vocation in Ireland is in direct proportion to the freedoms now accorded to single men and women. When my mother struck out in the world as a determinedly single woman, therefore, she was called upon to exhibit a strength of will which was truly remarkable in that era.

From the first, my mother was at all times elegant in her dress and precise in her manners, and held her head high as if daring others to judge her. I may have inherited her fastidiousness, but will not pretend to any of her courage. Her qualities, however, were not recognised in the types of employment open to her. As an only child she had been afforded the advantages of a good education: but a woman was still at a disadvantage when applying for a job appropriate to her qualifications. And my mother was too proud to take a job she felt to be 'beneath' her. So instead, some short months after my father's passing, she threw herself into a study of the financial markets, taking her inheritance and investing it widely and wisely in a variety of high-yield investments. No doubt she suffered reversals as well as successes over that period; but all in all she proved a skilled trader, managing to grow her income and the value of her investments several times over, in the course of several decades. It is my understanding from documents passed on to me after her death that she 'cashed out' all of these early in the year 2000, shortly before the stock market crash, and this divestment may have had something to do with the extra time she found to devote to other interests. Suffice to say that the estate she left me is sufficient for someone of my modest needs - if less than my former wife's lawyers would attest. In this I am reminded of one of my mother's favourite adages: "The best revenge is living well."

May Burke, it can be inferred, was self-sufficient in all the ways you might expect. If she had any romantic attachments during those years I was unaware of them, and I suspect that if she had, this would not be the first memoir to be published by someone with a claim to knowing her well.

Her experience on the Dan Crowley show should have steeled her for her subsequent encounters with the press. But they too had learned from that experience. As determined as she might have been to maintain an even temper, they had also been alerted to the news-value of provoking her into some impassioned outburst. When she agreed to speak out following the deaths of the Cuddys and the Flemings, they set about her with sharp sticks.

The fact that she had agreed to an interview had in itself excited much interest. She had discovered that far from people's fascination with her subsiding, maintaining her silence merely served to entrench the view that she was some kind of mastermind, or in some way culpable for what had happened. Wary of facing another ratings-chasing 'journo', she agreed to go on RTE's Prime Time show, on the understanding that the program would focus on the mistreatment of the elderly and that she would be merely one of those to be interviewed. The Flemings had posted a video on YouTube (following the example of Islamic terrorists, it was claimed) explaining the reasons for their actions and again calling for the rights of elders to be recognised and addressed. They went further than the Cuddys, however, in calling on others to join their protest. It has been argued interminably whether they had intended others to follow their example, or merely to support their cause. But the point is moot. What followed was doubtlessly shaped by their actions… but it is equally clear that my mother's words acted as a further, if not the vital, catalyst.

The format of Prime Time involves an introductory video, followed by a panel discussion. Typically, as many as three or four different topics are covered in each one-and-a-half-hour program, broadcast each Thursday night at 9:00pm to an audience of between 700,000 and 900,000 people.

Given that the entire population of Ireland is a little under 5,000,000, this is a not inconsiderable number. I do not know the exact figure for the broadcast of February 11th, but it is reasonable to expect that the numbers were at the higher reaches of this estimate, given public interest in the topic. That level of interest can also be gauged from the fact that, on this occasion, it was the sole topic under consideration.

The opening video was everything my mother might have wished: balanced, thorough, with reference to the Lees Tribunal and interviews with current residents of old folks' homes alongside public representatives, and relatives of those affected by previous scandals. The picture they painted was one of systematic neglect and inadequate controls, and the filmmakers sought to broaden the discussion by highlighting what it viewed as examples of profiteering by named owners of private care homes in Limerick and Cork cities.

My mother was joined on the panel by Junior Minister for Justice Miriam Cavanaugh, the Lord Mayor of Dublin, Alderman John Byrne, and Evie Macmillan from Age Concern. Although Myles Kingston directed his first question to Evie Macmillan - who outlined in detail the range of discriminatory practices and state failures in regard to the welfare of senior citizens - it quickly became apparent that the debate would focus upon the effect, rather than the cause, of the extraordinary events of recent weeks. Perhaps the extreme and very public nature of those deaths made such an emphasis unavoidable. Alderman Byrne – though taking care to note his sympathies for all involved – described the impact the deaths had had upon traffic and tourism as "catastrophic". Minister Cavanaugh, in response to a question about the legality of such actions, made it clear that any attempt to emulate Mary Connolly, the Careys or the Flemings could lead to arrest for a range of offences up to and including reckless endangerment, which was subject to imprisonment. When asked why her ministry rather than that of Health was being represented that evening, her response was half hearted at best. Mrs Macmillan, a well-meaning but politically inexperienced campaigner followed the general trend of the argument while trying to elicit some concession toward additional government funding. From the moment Kingston introduced the debate with the phrase "We need no reminding of the terrible events of recent days" my mother sat there in a simmering rage. That rage – despite the assurances to the contrary she had given me as I drove her to Montrose – would soon boil over. To her, it seemed that those deaths were being treated as threats to public safety rather than as the ultimate expression of her constituency's outrage and despair. Having remained silent for as long as she could, believing that she should respect the format of the discussion, she eventually felt compelled to speak.

"I'm sorry - but why should we care about the smooth flow of traffic in our capital when a good proportion of its citizens are living in such terrible conditions that they would consider taking their own lives?"

"I don't think we can divorce their actions from the consequences," replied Minister Cavanaugh.

"Quite," said my mother. "But frankly, I don't give a damn. I don't give a damn whether those same people who have ignored and mistreated older members of this society are stuck in traffic for an extra hour on their way home. I don't give a damn if tourists in their millions stay away from this false dream of Ireland you and your ilk continue to peddle. I have sat here and listened while you have complained about the noise of the trains bearing Jews to Auschwitz."

Her comments had the effect you would expect.

"That is outrageous!" said Byrne. "We are all of us sympathetic to the difficulties facing our senior citizens, but to-"

"What nonsense! And who do you imagine wants your "sympathies" Mr Byrne? The suggestion that you or Minister Cavanaugh here have any understanding of the plight of older people is not simply untrue, but insulting. When is the last time you were bustled over on a pavement? Or had your income reduced without notice, or redress? When did you last sit alone in a cold room deciding whether to spend the remaining pittance of your pension on food, or heat? Have you been force-fed? Or bullied by people younger and stronger than you, away from the view of anyone who might intervene – knowing full well that even if you did complain you would not be believed? Please wait, Minister, you've had your turn. Platitudes and condescension are not enough. Not any longer."

"Forgive me Mrs Burke, but that could be interpreted as a threat", interjected the host, Kingston.

"Well – wouldn't that be something! The very notion that older people could 'threaten' the rest of society! That they could demand that you listen to them! Was that not the aim of the poor souls who pursued such dreadful means to gain your attention? And fobbing them off, or giving dire warnings about their being imprisoned so that commuters can sail safely home in time for the evening news, is just not good enough!"

"Are we to take it then, Mrs Burke," Kingston asked, "that you condone their actions?"

I wonder at that moment if my mother realised the trap into which she had been lured? Looking back, you can see her pause. But the nature of a television debate is to disallow silence and to pressure panellists to respond.

"I think we can all agree that nobody should have to take such drastic action in order to gain the public's attention. Although it would be wrong to condone their actions, I think we can understand them. But no act of protest should endanger others, or put their safety at risk. As abhorrent as you might view their actions, we should also recognise that they were in every instance careful to minimise the potential danger to those around them. And, as unpalatable as you might find this, the fact is that discussions of this kind would not have taken place if they had not pursued such dire means. When is the last time the treatment of older members of our society has featured in one of your programs, Mr Kingston? Or been reflected in your policies,

Minister? The Lees Report is ten years old - and nothing has changed."

"I appreciate your passion, Mrs Burke – but I think you have a responsibility, here, to ensure that you are not encouraging others to follow in their footsteps as it were." The Minister's face had assumed a cold, hard expression, as if she were trying to browbeat my mother into a retraction. But as I said, they did not know her.

"I would suggest that the responsibility is yours, Minister. The continued failure of your government and previous administrations to address the concerns of older members of our society has been a direct cause of these deaths – and I feel that accusation is justified, despite your attempt to appear outraged. And as long as you continue to focus on the effects of those protests, rather than on the underlying causes, I have no doubt that you will see further protests. The question should not be what has to be done to stop it - but what will they have to do before you take their concerns seriously?"

The program ended shortly afterwards, the host having done what he could in the final minutes to add a dignified coda to events. I remember my mother getting into the car afterwards with a face like murder, not even deigning to reply when I jokingly said "Well, that went well!"

The interpretation of the words she used is obviously of importance in looking back upon my mother's life. It is perhaps apposite to acknowledge that words are used by Irish people in ways often dissimilar to those of other English-speaking nations. I have heard the Irish comedian Paul Howell explain those differences in terms of music, with words serving as notes. In one of his routines he gave the example of the father of a teenage girl reaction to her coming downstairs dressed in a tight-fitting top, and what might be described as either a very undersized skirt or a slightly oversized belt.

"An American father would tell her "Get back upstairs and change." Simple, clear and unequivocal. Americans speak an English which is like the blues. It's short, plain, and full of the same endlessly repeated phrases. Like, you know? An English father on the other hand, would add some form of formal address. "Get straight back upstairs this minute and change, young lady!" Young Lady! She's your daughter! What do you call your wife? Madam? "I wonder, madam, if oral sex might be on the list of available services this eventide?" But that's the English for you. They speak the language like it's a form of martial music. Every word must be lined up in step, in a particular order, and any command issued should sound like one, and include the correct appellation. And God forbid you allow any word to step out of line, or take another's position! It's ironic, isn't it, that the English defeated the Germans, but only one of those nations still harbours Grammar Nazis!

"Ireland's relationship to the language is more like jazz. You'll find the same words in there somewhere, but we're inclined to change the rhythm as we feel like it, and to introduce other seemingly unconnected words as and when the fancy takes us. In this case, rather than a straightforward command, you can expect an Irish father to ask a rhetorical question, along with some surreal juxtaposition of anatomy and attire: "If you think you're going out *in them legs*, then you have another think coming!"

Most amusing: but I digress. Sufficient to say, my mother's words were rarely open to misinterpretation. She chose those she used with great care, and seldom used one without purpose.

What might her intention have been, then, in refusing to issue a condemnation? Was it a deliberate omission, or merely a response to the badgering of the host and her fellow panellists? I have no doubt that she found the actions taken by those who had died up to that date abhorrent – but she believed it would have been disrespectful of their memory to condemn their methods without first addressing the substance of their protest. The cause, as she had put it, rather than the effect.

What we mean and what is heard are often distant cousins. Press and public opinion in the aftermath of the Prime Time broadcast coalesced around two themes. Firstly, that my mother had not only endorsed such actions, but used the program to issue a thinly-veiled threat of more to come. And secondly, that she had provided clear guidelines to any of her followers who might make good upon that threat. A code of practice, if you will, prohibiting any act which might place others in danger. If you are to accept any of this as true then you must accept that while my mother can be viewed as responsible for the loss of many more lives, she must also be credited with ensuring that number was kept to a minimum.

I remember our sitting together at the kitchen table that evening, eating in silence. My mother appeared drawn; exhausted, even.

"You should go to bed, mother," I eventually said, as the minutes passed and the look of strain upon her face deepened.

"And what good would that do, Dominic?" she replied, irritated. "Do you think I could sleep after that debacle?"

"Be that as it may," I said, firmly. "You need the rest at any rate. You are not young, mother – whatever exception you may take to that remark. And you need to conserve your energies. I do not doubt that this evening's broadcast will prove fodder for tomorrow's papers, and you will need to be at your best to weather the coming storm."

She looked back at me with what I could only surmise was shock at this unusual display of resolve, and slowly raised herself from her seat, proceeding from the kitchen upstairs to bed.

It was at that moment, I think, that I recognised how old she had become, and how much of a sap upon her energies all of this was to prove. It would be the first time she would accept my assistance, and would mark a sea-change in our relationship. Perhaps I had also realised what lay before us. Either way, having brought her up a last cup of tea and made sure that she was settled abed, I too broke the pattern of a lifetime and spent the rest of that evening cleaning the house. From that point on I was effectively her caretaker, much as she would have railed against that depiction, and did everything in my power to help her to conserve her energies. This was a duty most often performed in silence, but I like to think that she appreciated my efforts and was gratified to observe the change in my demeanour. Though I suspect Laura would have fainted quite away to see me on my knees cleaning a toilet bowl!

FOUR

The mystery in all this is why there was such resistance to their demands. Most of the legislators whose support they sought were either at or approaching the same age as the protestors, and simple self-interest should have made them sympathetic to their cause. That old white men would ignore the call of other old white men seems to defy logic. But ignore them they did. Perhaps the equating of these acts of public suicide with terrorism had a part to play here, given governments' habitual refusal to negotiate with terrorists. Or perhaps, as more cynical minds have suggested, it was simply the cost to the public purse of improving even one of the services to the aged by one half of one percent, and the electoral consequences which would accompany any rise in taxation to fund such reforms, which explained their resistance. At this point, of course, elders were still laying suit to the existing political parties, rather than forming their own.

Even more puzzling, of course, is why so many elderly people would adopt such extreme measures in order to make their voices heard. The notion that older people somehow hold life less dear has been widely discredited. If anything, it appears, the passing of the years makes each subsequent one more precious. There were, no doubt, some amongst the three thousand who were suffering from deep depressions, or who acted out in the wake of some tragedy or psychic upheaval. It has subsequently been revealed that a number of those who took their lives were suffering from incurable or chronic illnesses, though it is not always clear that they were aware of this fact. Awe and bemusement seem appropriate responses, in the absence of understanding. We must add to this – distasteful as it may appear – an acceptance that at some stage a spirit of competition seems to have taken hold of some of those involved. How else can we explain the escalation in the numbers who engaged in mass suicides, or the increasingly elaborate and, yes, imaginative means many of them employed? For some of these, the desire to shock seemed to accompany if not to outweigh the desire to register a protest.

But let us remind ourselves of the conditions they were protesting against. Conditions which, as my mother said, were often worse than inhumane. What is the difference, the question goes, between an old folks' home and a prison? Answer: prisoners get visitors. Of course, that's no longer true - but we should remind ourselves of what life was like for older members of our society at that time. Isolation. Neglect. Depression and despair. Emotional, financial, medical, physical and yes, even sexual abuse. Residents in approved nursing homes were regularly ignored, denied normal hygiene and wellness assistance, forced to sleep on dirty sheets and left untreated whether their needs were for basic dental care, treatment of bedsores, or for chronic illnesses such as diabetes. Eight in ten instances of elder abuse went unreported. Whereas the public could be roused to action at the very thought of child abuse, the tormenting of people often returned to a second childhood – helpless, dependent, guiltless of malice – was ignored, as were they, and the injuries they suffered were seldom exposed or addressed. Every day these people were robbed, bullied and demeaned, and society as a whole could not have cared less. In many cases even their closest relatives – their own children – seemed happy to turn a blind eye, dreading the very possibility of having to undertake the burden of housing them under their own roof, or the inconvenience of finding them an alternative residential facility. I worry that we may forget what conditions were like then. But it is necessary, I feel, to understand that stories of such abuse were being fed to my mother each and every day. They reached her via her website. Via email. Often via mail, the letters arriving in the post in increasing numbers as if she were some lotto winner being sued for donations. They were in front of her eyes and ears every day, cited in press articles and radio and TV broadcasts in the aftermath of each public suicide. After a while, I took to hiding the volume of letters from her, though I suspect she was aware of the part I played in editing her mountain of correspondence. For what could she do? How could one woman right a litany of historic wrongs, or intervene in cases where the abuse was taking place behind the closed doors of their own homes? Faced with such a deluge of misery and fear, of sickening violence and cruelty, the only choice left to her lay between despair, and anger.

These were strange days for us. Subjected to a bombardment of attention from public and press alike whilst out and about, our home life to the contrary was remarkably serene, differing only in my fledgling efforts to make more of a contribution to domestic tasks. We sat together each morning over the newspapers, my mother with a bowl of porridge and some fruit and I with some whole-wheat toast liberally spread with good Seville Orange marmalade, and discussed the day's itinerary. As I fulfilled the role of chauffeur as well as housekeeper, it was important to ensure that our calendars were synchronised. Afterwards, we would each retire to our respective bedrooms to dress for the day ahead, spending whatever time was required before putting a face before the public. One of my few remaining vices was a passion for double-cuffed shirts and good cufflinks, and I indulged myself with the purchase of some choice examples of the latter during this time, using the excuse of my new-found celebrity. I was never more than a figure in the background, of course, but the excuse functioned well enough. We performed these preparations without ever discussing the purpose of our daily engagements. Every meeting or event was planned for in the same manner, whether this was a visit to a constituency office or a rally in some public park. What and when. Never why.

Much as I'd like to say that I felt resentful about this, or thirsted after some emotional 'coming together', the reality is that I was as happy to keep things on a practical basis as she was. I am not sure I could have borne the weight of being her confessor -

and even if she felt the need of such I doubt she would have thought me up to the task. Those rallies and public gatherings were growing in number and in size. Often organized in the aftermath of a funeral, they provided my mother with a platform for her views and solidified her status as the public face of the protest. It helped that she was a fiery orator, able to convey opprobrium and determination within a single sentence. Obviously, practice played a part, but she would have been determined in any case never to let herself down by employing a clumsy turn of phrase.

Ironically, it wasn't another instance of elder abuse or a further loss of life which pushed things to the next level, but a small act of defiance. For a brief period in late March my mother's celebrity was eclipsed by a man of eighty-two's.

Clem Fletcher was a pensioner living in one of the last remaining homes run by the religious orders, just outside of Wexford Town. He survived on what was left of his military pension, a gift from the state whose value had declined less rapidly than most linked as it was to the schemes offered to senior public servants. He spent his allowance on the staples of a decent life. Namely good shirts and neckties, and a pint of Guinness each evening in his local pub, where his quiet manner was welcomed and his name was known. I often feel that such establishments – despite the poor reputation they enjoy amongst those of a puritan persuasion – act as vital links to the community for pensioners like Clem. He was left in peace there, perched on his usual stool at the end of the bar with the evening paper spread out before him, but his custom was valued and he was never ignored, nor denied a warm greeting and a kindly word from proprietor and regulars alike. Clem always paid for his first pint, but usually left having drunk two.

It was their misfortune then when two young men decided to stop in at Finnegan's to buy the next in what was clearly a series of drinks, and objected to the amount of counter space taken up by Clem's Evening Herald. It took him a second or two to realise what the "Do you mind?" issuing from the taller of the young men referred to but, ever the gent, he quickly apologised and folded the paper so as not to encroach upon them.

Clem's recollection was less than exact on the details of the remarks which subsequently passed between them, but it appears they attempted to amuse themselves by asking him a series of increasingly profane and embarrassing questions with regard to the nightlife in the locale, and the conviviality of the local maidens. Had Dave Pegman the proprietor not been below stairs changing a keg, there is little doubt that their antics would have been quickly curtailed, as would have been the case if any of the regulars had been in earshot. As it was, Clem felt compelled to take them to task himself.

"That's enough lads. Do yourselves a favour, okay?"

And it is at this point that a simple encounter in a public bar segues into something emblematic of a shift in the very culture. According to Clem, he would ordinarily have been content to ride out their jibes and to ignore their provocations. But, emboldened by the actions of his contemporaries in recent weeks (by the very fact that people of his age were on the front page of his newspaper, he said) he took it further. When the taller of the two put an arm about him in a condescending manner, laughing as he mimicked his rejoinder, Clem reached down to steady himself upon his stool before bringing his arm up sharply elbow-first, the point of it connecting with the young man's nose and sending him staggering backwards. When his companion jumped up from his seat and appeared primed to advance upon him, Clem planted the left toe of a black brogue firmly between the shorter man's legs, causing him to buckle and heave the contents of the day's festivities upon the tiled floor. At no point had Clem left his seat.

A customer had whipped out his mobile phone on hearing the initial commotion and managed to catch Clem's confrontation with the second man, the first still visible in the foreground clutching his bloody nose and issuing a high-pitched and plaintive wail. What is perhaps most remarkable about the footage is Clem's composure. As one journalist put it (Clem's copy of The Evening Herald having been clearly visible upon the bar, he was inevitably the subject of a follow-up article under the headline 'Elderly Herald Reader Tackles Thugs') he appeared utterly unconcerned. "As calm and confident as Spenser Tracy in 'Bad Day at Blackrock'." I am sure there was a sub-editor somewhere lamenting the fact that this encounter had not taken place a few steps further along the DART line - but the point was well made, and was soon translated into a broader context. The elderly, it was clear, were no longer happy to cower in silence. And if respect was not automatically given them, then they would demand it.

Thanks in large part to the internet, rather than press coverage, Clem became something of a cause celebre. And as the 'poster-grandad' for a new movement, he was ideally suited. Soft spoken.

Thoughtful. Neatly dressed. Despite being several inches shorter than his height as a young man, he was still an impressive figure: his back ramrod straight and his broad if thin shoulders far from slumped. As befitted a former Irish Ranger who had served several tours in The Lebanon. It is doubtful the two 'thugs' could have picked a worse target. But Clem Fletcher had an importance well beyond his own story. Public perception of the aged was now viewed through a lens which depicted his generation as formidable, rather than helpless. Strong of purpose, and up for a fight. Secretly, I suspect my mother hated him.

The press however loved him. Stories and features about the aged had increased in number during that period, with Image Magazine even dedicating an entire issue to what they termed 'the third age', with articles on fashion for the over-sixties ('Ageless Beauty') and interviews with prominent personalities including a Rolling Stone, a well-known female novelist and a seventy-five-year-old surfer with an impossibly toned physique who had become something of a celebrity amongst the surfing fraternity both here and in the United States ('Pension My A*s!'). It is hard to assess at this remove whether Clem Fletcher was correct in identifying a new-found respect for the old, which he claimed lay behind his act of courage. But that spirit of defiance would soon extend elsewhere, and violence would once again prove a factor.

But I am getting ahead of myself. I should first address the impact of events overseas. It bears restating that it was not foreign nationals at this juncture but Irish citizens, who extended the protest beyond our shores. Just as our ancestors sailed forth to teach the uneducated masses in medieval times, and civilised societies from Bohemia to Bolivia, so the diaspora adopted our latest export and brought what the Americans took to calling "The Granny Suicides" to other nations. Paris was first; but then the French have always been enamoured of obscure philosophies. So it proved when three tourists contrived to make their grand gesture atop the most symbolic of Parisian buildings. Three old women - two lifelong friends and a more recent confrere who had fallen in with the others during their years together in the local John Player 'Talk of the town' amateur dramatic troupe.

There was more than a touch of the dramatic to how they staged their grand statement. Apparently, their original plan had been to wait until July 14th when their protest would seem most apposite, but the failing health of one of their party and the likely increase in police presence which would accompany a public holiday convinced them to accelerate their timetable.

Place Saint Michel was being dug up, as usual, pedestrian traffic squeezed between the roadway and the remaining narrow width of pavement to the left of the square as the usual tourists and winos gathered about the base of the fountain of the sword-wielding angel, and yappy dogs strained on their leads as owners from the locale stopped to exchange news. The early evening sun was setting behind Place Saint Andre, the last insipid rays illuminating the zinc roofs and the windscreens of traffic heading across the river to the Ile de la Cite. Pigeons swooped past the 5th floor balconies, passing over the heads of headphone-wearing teens with backpacks and neck scarfs, black-clad citizens scurrying home from work, and the occasional couple wheeling their first and likely last child in a buggy. There were maybe six or seven hundred people in all in the immediate proximity of the fountain, though that number would increase rapidly from the moment one of them spotted a middle-aged woman take her perilous stance upon the rosette of stone atop the heraldic shield at the very uppermost point.

It was not so much that she was standing there, but how she was dressed which first excited people's interest. Her hair was long and free flowing over her shoulders. The dress she wore was a voluminous one dating from a previous epoch, the faded gold skirt topped by a black sash and the bodice loosened and lowered to reveal one breast. The tableau was immediately recognisable by any French person above the age of two, and most of them assumed this was intended as a form of street art - like those performers who spray themselves gold or silver and effect the stillness of statues in order to elicit donations from people sufficiently impressed by an ability to stand stock still upon a wooden box in the midst of a teeming thoroughfare. Unbeknownst to them, this same homage to Delacroix's portrait of Liberty was being repeated at Place de la Concorde from a top floor bedroom at the Hotel de Crillon, and on the parapet of the Basilica of St Denis, each of the three women similarly attired and exposed, and each carrying a pole which they unfurled to reveal a replica of the revolutionary flag with one of the words Liberte, Egalite and Fraternite respectively overlaid in black. No image could be more evocative or more likely to be seized upon by a newspaper editor in search of an image for the following day's front page. And this was before they jumped, and the lengths of white rope they had hidden beneath their skirts reached their maximum length, halting their descent courtesy of the nooses tucked about their throats and leaving these macabre mannequins to swing back and forth before the monumental backdrops, the flagpoles they had carefully stitched into the folds of the clothes remaining erect and proclaiming the virtues of a previous revolution to the stunned onlookers below… a goodly percentage of whom were taking and sharing pictures of what they witnessed, causing an effective collapse of social media as the complementary images joined them, and the level of orchestration became apparent. There was outrage of course at this appropriation of French iconography; but also admiration, not just for the principles the three women had espoused in such a radical fashion, but for the glorious theatre it represented. The headline in La Republique the following day, above a triptych of the three women taken moments before their fatal plunge, was 'En attendant God', a nod to another Irishman whose dramatic ambitions had been realised in the French capital. In a way they were right, of course. It was just the sort of gesture one could imagine Beckett applauding for its nihilism, wry humour and stagecraft. All three sites offered comparatively easy access, in contrast to more historically significant sites such as the Concierge, which in the years since it was used to house almost three thousand prisoners of the revolution, including Marie Antoinette herself prior to her execution, since functioned as an official building for the department of justice.

The images would circulate around the globe. The American and European Press - who had devoted feature articles to the spate of suicides in Ireland while still regarding it as a national phenomenon - now openly questioned whether the protest would reach beyond the shores of that small island and bring mayhem and horror to their own communities, the story of these elderly martyrs no longer a feature story but front page news. And my mother in her turn – as the available focal point for this extraordinary movement – became a global figure, and the subject of enquiry and outrage.

To give her her due, she did not shirk from the attention. Meaner minds might accredit this to an opportunity to resume the spotlight, following Clem Fletcher's brief moment of fame, but I prefer to believe that she felt compelled to speak up for those who could not, an obligation others were either unwilling or unable to assume. Hers would not be the only eloquent voice of protest raised in the coming weeks, however. Nor, indeed, the most famous.

FIVE

Cheryl is suspending her @therealCherylWinters account and extends her love & best wishes to all her followers. www.youtube.com/eu65e78256c3

An innocuous enough message, and following a pattern used by celebrities such as Stephen Fry and James Franco when their accounts became the locus of hate speak or personal abuse in the wake of some social or political indiscretion. No such faux pas predated the six-times Oscar winning actress (or actor, as we are instructed to call female performers nowadays). Unlike many of her contemporaries she had not retained her place in the public eye by adopting some cause of the day, or assuming a role as a goodwill ambassador to raise awareness of some global health or education challenge once the meaty roles had dried up. In fact, her career had undergone something of an autumnal renaissance of recent times, with significant parts in three award-winning movies and a best supporting actor nomination (her first) in one of these, all within a calendar year. Her greatest performance, however, had been reserved for the three-minute video to which that innocuous link at the end of her final 'tweet' directed her followers.

The clip – as you no doubt recall - opens with Cheryl on 5th Avenue just across from the Rockefeller Center, its vainglorious statuary visible over her right shoulder. She is wearing a headscarf and sunglasses in an imitation of Jackie Kennedy which puts all previous screen portrayals to shame. She is, as ever, fabulous. Her disguise appears to be effective however as no one stops to accost her with a request for an autograph or, woe of woes, a 'selfie', a situation no doubt helped by the large numbers of people pausing to take photographs of the landmark across the busy street.

She smiles and addresses the camera, which she places a few feet away atop a municipal rubbish bin.

"My dear friends. In a few moments my assistant, Jane Seymour – no, not that one – will arrive to collect this video, having been instructed to come here immediately via a message I left on her phone some moments back. The instructions I gave her were to collect this camera from its current position, providing some opportunist does not steal it in the melee shortly to commence, and to upload the contents to my social media accounts before the day is out. As a failsafe I have left a number of letters detailing the reasons for my actions with certain of my friends and professional acquaintances. I am here, I am sorry to announce, to say a final goodbye. I am not sad to part, but very sad indeed to leave you - my friends and fans, whose love has lifted and supported me throughout my long career and in all facets of my life. Thank you! Thank You! Thank you! I am not ill, nor in any financial or emotional difficulty, but for the past few weeks I have not been able to get the situation facing women – and men – above my own age in this cold and often thankless world from my mind. The acts of bravery we have seen from elders in Europe have stunned and shocked me, as I am sure they have you. But the cause for which they laid down their lives is still ignored, and the mistreatment of our senior population shows no sign of ending. That is why I have decided to add my voice to those demanding change. In the words of Mahatma Gandhi, to be the change we want in the world. Be good. Be kind. And know that I carry you all in my heart." And with that, careful as ever to remain centred in shot, she stepped out into the insanity of Manhattan traffic.

What most people did not spot, so practiced was she at cinematic sleight of hand, was that she had swallowed two capsules as she turned to walk away.

Capsules later revealed to contain deadly amounts of a fast-acting poison whose name was withheld due to its extreme efficacy, although it is rumoured to be a substance often used in that community to promote rapid weight loss (albeit in smaller quantities). In the event, she need not have worried. Traffic in Manhattan at the hour she chose for her grand gesture was light, but typically aggressive, and thus it was that a Dimitri Landis ended her life instantaneously whilst attempting to pass another yellow cab by speeding through on the inner lane just as she stepped from the pavement. The photo of her sunglasses lying broken but upright on the tarmac would grace the front pages of a thousand tabloid newspapers the following day.

The death of a celebrity excited considerably more attention than the deaths of housewives and notaries on distant shores. Although my mother refused invitations to appear on various news outlets and talk shows (although she did briefly consider appearing on The Ellen Show) the story rapidly developed a momentum of its own, with clips of her previous speeches and interviews liberally employed to provide distraught viewers with some context for Cheryl's actions. The shock waves, as they invariably call them, spread throughout the English-speaking world. #CherylNo and #CherylHero became the most active 'trends' on social media and facilitated a virtual war between those who viewed the actor as a misguided fool who had set a dangerous example and those who viewed her as a latter-day martyr, making the ultimate sacrifice in the spirit of Martin Luther King, Bobby Kennedy, or Christ himself. As ever, shades of grey were difficult to detect.

The situation facing the elderly in the United States was, admittedly, torrid. Whereas elder members of society might be ignored or side-lined in European countries they at least had recourse to some form of national health service to furnish their most basic needs, including food and housing. Not so in many parts of the USA. Those without the means to enjoy a comfortable retirement were effectively abandoned, dependent on the charity of relatives and their local church or community organizations, who in that country assume much of the burden repudiated by taxpayers and their elected representatives. I have heard it said that if it were proven that an extra cent in taxes could fund a cure for both cancer and global warming, a majority of Americans would actively court melanomas and spend additional time in the sun rather than deplete their personal finances by one such iota. Nowhere, it appears, was the disparity between the rich and the poor more evident than amongst those dependent upon assisted living, as it is known over there. 'Poolside Or Roadside' was how one commentator described it.

Accompanying the plethora of reports about Cheryl's career and legacy, and features about the treatment and circumstances of seniors, was an unspoken fear. Though everyone was thinking it, the networks had adopted a policy of ignoring the danger of so-called 'copycat' suicides, reasoning that even to discuss the possibility could increase the likelihood of such occurrences. For three fraught days (until the death of a rock superstar consigned Cheryl to the newsworthy past) the US appeared to hold its breath. And on the 3rd day the floodgates opened.

SIX

Everything is bigger in America. Or so they claim. In this case it proved both true and untrue. Yes, we saw more instances of elders committing suicide than had been the case up to that point in Europe. But looked at purely statistically, in terms of size of population, there were less suicides per 100,000 people (which is apparently how they measure such things) than on the other side of the Atlantic.

This may in part have been because the suicide rate amongst elders was already so high. The rate of attempted suicide for men in particular was on the rise and – perhaps due to their greater experience, and the reasoned way they went about it – the rates of success were higher than amongst younger men.

Veterans were a group who already scored above the norm in these grisly league tables, and it was no surprise to see them disproportionately represented in the numbers of those who died in the immediate wake of Cheryl Winters' death. Access to weapons, a history of commitment to a cause, preexisting PTSD or depression… all of these were cited as contributory factors. What seems undeniable is that their allegiances – and rivalries – contributed to the All-American spirit of competition which soon prevailed.

Ironically, perhaps the most informed press coverage from that time came from the satirical magazine The Onion. It ran a national 'poll' allowing its readers to vote on what they thought the 'best' method employed by the estimated two hundred and eleven people who took their lives in the month immediately following Cheryl's 'passing', as the euphemism has it. At first, a casual reader might assume that these were fictional - typical examples of the hyperbole employed in most of The Onion's articles. But as we know, this was not the case. Three decorated marines really did blow themselves up using World War II munitions whilst inside a tank from the same era, which they had managed to drive onto Pennsylvania Avenue. Apparently their efforts were celebrated by younger servicemen in bases across the nation, in much the same way as Lee Harvey Oswald's marksmanship is celebrated by the Corps. Not to be outdone, two former Airforce lieutenants dive-bombed a remote airstrip in Dublin, Ohio. It wasn't until news helicopters arrived to survey the wreckage for the local news channels that the enormous red, white and blue target they had 'painted' on the runway using elderly water trucks filed with dye became visible. Needless to say, they had scored a perfect bullseye. For over a week – once the connection between these events became known – the public held its breadth to see what the Navy would come up with in response. As John Oliver noted in his weekly news show, it had become a matter of national pride that they do so, rather than an outcome to be desired that they would refrain. In veterans' associations across the country it was claimed that naval personnel could not hold their heads high in company until the hiatus was ended by Rear Admiral Augustus Dunaway, the highest ranking of all the veterans to end their lives and arguably the most inventive, who commandeered a tourist launch off Tampa Bay at gunpoint with a large rucksack in his other hand, ordering all of the passengers to alight and driving it at speed directly toward the McDill Air Force Base, having informed the coast guard by radio that he had explosives armed with detonators on board. Thus ensuring that two F-22 Raptor fighter planes were scrambled, and deployed their cargo of AIM 9 Sidewinder missiles to prevent his reaching the costal base, and blowing the tourist craft an estimated thirty feet from the water. It is said that members of both the Navy and Air Force raised a glass to the Rear Admiral that evening, his efforts effecting a rapprochement between these two wings of the armed services.

Veterans were not the only ones to take their lives, of course. Professions from schoolteachers to dental hygienists, from civic engineers to so-called captains of industry were represented in the roll of the fallen. One anomaly which did emerge was the disproportionate number of democrats rather than republicans amongst that number: a disparity the former put down to their constituents' greater concern about social issues, and which the latter put down to superior powers of reason.

Nor were the veterans alone in employing creative means to bring their lives to a premature end. We think of the three friends who leaped off the fifteenth-highest building in Chicago using outsized American flags as 'parachutes', memorably slowing, if not stalling, their descent. Or the Arkansas couple in their eighties who celebrated their Diamond Wedding anniversary by driving her not-quite-as-elderly 1952 Cadillac into the Little Missouri River at the Crater of Diamonds State Park in Murfreesboro, home of the world's only diamond-bearing site accessible to the public.

Most of the American suicides however were pathetic events. People broken or overcome by despair, or homelessness. Worn down by illness or depression and seeing in that moment an opportunity to end their suffering and to contribute their voice to a louder clamour for attention to the needs of those like them. Because behind all of this invention, of course, was a persistent issue. One people were prepared to give up their lives to highlight; and hopefully to affect. The extraordinary rate of abuse and suicide amongst those in residential homes in particular was a national scandal as Linus Goodie, one such suicide, stated whilst outlining the reasons behind his own decision to terminate his life. In his case, he achieved this by taking a low-energy heater into his bath at a residential facility, or a senior living center as it was euphemistically called. The litany of abuses he was subject to prior to his death, which he detailed in a letter to the local press, makes for sobering reading. These were largely insidious: covert, rather than overt. The use of excessive force when bathing him or 'assisting' him to bed, or to his chair in the lunchroom or anteroom. Yelling at him in front of other residents, a source of deep humiliation for him. Ignoring his requests for help, often for hours on end. Shoving him aside on the corridor during his morning exercise, once sending his cane flying across the floor and forcing him to prop himself against a wall while he sought to retrieve it. Making fun of him and of his frailties, adding to the indignity he already suffered as a result of having to wear incontinence pants. Using language he found distasteful, and often insulting. A subsequent investigation discovered that the number of elders who had developed bed sores as a result of negligence comprised more than 40% of the most infirm patients.

It is extraordinary to us now that such cruel treatment could escape discovery, let alone censure. Few residents in homes such as this are now without monitoring equipment, or 'granny cams' as the devices are often termed. We find it difficult to imagine that individuals suffering from a variety of ailments would be confined to beds in a ward where infection could spread to disastrous effect and where the distress or manic behaviour of their bedfellows could make sleep or recuperation an impossibility. And, however loath we may be to think of such things, the question has to be asked whether anything would have changed were it not for the sacrifices made by men and women like Linus.

We lack the words, frankly, to address the injustices visited upon the old. In America, in our own country, and elsewhere. It beggars belief. Did it truly require mass suicides to draw attention to such mistreatment? Where were the controls – the checks and balances – which should have rendered such things impossible... or at the very least rare? How could a significant percentage of the population remain invisible and unheard? I, too, remain conflicted in my view of the actions taken by those who used public recklessness to demand our attention. Were such actions truly necessary? Were there no other avenues of recourse which they might have employed, which would have spared their lives and spared us the horrific scenes which played out upon our streets and in our local communities? Was this, as some have suggested, a form of collective madness, a self-perpetuating nightmare which extended well past the effort to draw attention to the issues at hand? Were older people to some extent revelling in the power they had acquired over the rest of us: to intimidate, to horrify, to coerce? There are some, we know, who would level a similar charge against them even now.

SEVEN

Although there were attempts to seize the limelight from my mother (by opportunists and religious zealots mainly) the press quickly linked these latest deaths to her campaign. And as the press in the US is considerably less temperate – and virtually unregulated – the stories they printed about her were oftentimes not simply sensationalist, but downright slanderous. Opinion was sharply divided. Rolling Stone magazine made her their person of the year. The more moderate amongst the established broadsheets sought to place the events in context, and devoted a laudable amount of space to the issues underlying these protests, leading one investigative team to win the Pulitzer Prize for exposing rampant abuse by homes run by a religious order, who managed to add indoctrination and the denial of privilege to their crimes whilst enforcing a culture of religious adherence. Along with the usual evils. Other publications, however, were less even-handed. "Duchess of Death" (a somewhat inflated description given our family origins). "Granny Genocide" (which I was not alone in thinking employed far too many syllables for their typical reader). The most common description was "evil"; as in "this evil woman" or "the evil mastermind behind", etc. My mother rightly took umbrage with all of these labels - but in hindsight I suspect she had already begun to reflect on her own part in the events which had transpired over the course of the few short months since her appearance on the Dan Crowley show. Things, clearly, were out of control.

The good news however was that politicians in all of the countries affected (which soon included Greece, Italy - including most memorably the Vatican State - and most of the Scandinavian countries.. although given the high incidence of suicide in those parts these were adjudged to have less of an obvious correlation) began to mobilise. Nothing concentrates a politician's mind like the prospect of being turfed out of office. And given the fervour now surrounding the issue of the treatment of the elderly, they did not prove slow to jump aboard the bandwagon.

As ever, the positions they took were contrary ones. There were those who believed greater controls over the movements of the elderly were required in order to maintain 'public safety': and some who sought to address the issues the protesters insisted lay behind the sequence of these public suicides. France was among those who - initially at least - sought to control events via draconian measures, an approach driven by extreme right-wing parties in the Assemblée Nationale who characterized the elderly as another social grouping to be suspected, like the Romany people or immigrants in general, as being somehow 'un-French'. Any attempt to discriminate by age was impossible to enforce however, and doomed to failure. Particularly as many of the public officials, and the judiciary in particular, belonged to the target demographic! In the main, most nations sought to defuse the crisis by passing emergency legislation to appease the protesters, hoping to remove the incentive for such extreme behaviour.

I feel my mother has been given too little credit for the way in which she managed those negotiations here in Ireland. It would have been easy to accept the first sops to public opinion offered by the legislators, which in the main consisted of "tribunals' and 'committees of investigation'. Backed by an increasingly active and belligerent consistency – whose voice was finally being heard – she demanded far more significant concessions of them. It is hard not to spy naked self-interest in much of this. With such a large percentage of the electorate rallying behind a single issue, any politician viewed as supporting their cause would be virtually guaranteed a seat in any future election. So it was that the 'campaign for justice' moved from the streets to the floor of the Oireachtas, a transition mirrored in nation states across the western world. Such efforts would not be repeated in many less advanced nations, however, where the elderly were either ignored, as was the case with people who were gay or transgender, or in many cases - it must be admitted - already accorded the respect and support withheld from those in what we term the 'developed' world.

Most of the protections the elderly currently enjoy date from the three-month period between July and September 2016. The stringent regulatory practices to which all residential and care facilities were required to submit – and the formation of the Ministry for Older Citizens – were also established during this period.

But as we know, the suicides did not stop. August of that year saw the largest number of suicides to date, with over 500 people taking their lives in 21 different nations. In part this reflected the fact that many countries were still at the nascent stage of their national protests. And much has been written about the 'contribution' made by teens and young people in their twenties and thirties, who cited the mistreatment of the elderly and a wish to show their solidarity as a factor in their own decisions to commit suicide. I feel there is merit to the argument that many of these would have taken their lives regardless, and cannot so easily be attributed directly to The Elder Terror, as it was routinely described by that time. Nevertheless, the number of deaths was quite appalling. Particularly given the apparent progress being made by those, like my mother, who were successfully attempting to address their core concerns via peaceful means.

Given subsequent events, I should speak here of her state of mind. Although exhausted both physically and mentally by the events of recent months, she appeared newly energized during the period of the negotiations with the government. Something of the competitive nature of such discourses appealed to her on an intellectual level. I believe she saw herself as somehow emblematic of the intelligence and perspicacity of all those of her age, and viewed every dispute as a battle to be won for her consistency. If she could outflank and frustrate her opponent at the same time, even better. Years of bridge training had equipped her with both the patience and the strategic cunning required to sit in those meetings and to prevail, regardless of the experience of the people facing her across the table. She was also at this point a consummate media performer, taking renewed confidence from her success at the negotiation table. A number of the older - or more opportunistic - members of the opposition party had 'defected' to her cause, allowing her to share much of the burden of representing the interests of the aged at those same discussions, and allowing her to throw herself with renewed vigour into the public discourse being conducted in the media.

A new theme arose, however, once the legislature had convinced itself that it was addressing the issues the elderly had raised. Namely the morality of continuing these acts of 'terrorism' - and, by extension, my mother's complicity in these and subsequent deaths. The reversal was swift. Within days, my mother was being pressurized into asking for a cessation of hostilities, as it were, although fully understanding that she had no control over the individuals perpetuating the outrage. In truth, when it came to that particular group of the disaffected, she had no control at all. For what is suicide, after all, but a wresting of control from all but yourself? I think she realised at this juncture that an appeal for calm would have no effect. Worse, it could deprive her of any influence she might later exert. And so she declined, refusing perfectly reasonable requests to appeal for an end to the epidemic of suicides amongst the very people she claimed to represent - and was vilified as a result.

It was around this period that she began to confide in me. I suspect that she was abandoned by others in her inner circle, dismayed as they were at her failure to make any public statement. I think she was gratified, however, by both my continued, unquestioning support and my understanding. I shared as much with her - telling her my thoughts about the reasoning which must, I felt, lie behind her decision. And hearing me lay it out, as it were, she actually smiled at me. At my intelligence as much as my sympathy, I'd like to believe. Though I have no doubt that she took credit for the former and attributed it to her genes or childrearing skills. Such as they were! Regardless: I know that she was grateful to have me there, as the press once again laid siege to our home, and that time has an especial significance for me.

I'll admit, however, that I cannot identify the point at which she made her grand decision. She appeared unaltered to me during that final fortnight, whilst we were effectively holed up with only the phone and her laptop offering a connection with the outside world. But, in the event, they would be all that she needed. How vainglorious of the popular press to continue to regard themselves as the arbiters of public opinion! A sixteen-year-old can generate a larger readership by posting one witty video or a screen recording of himself whilst playing a video game. Older people may still buy 'the papers' - but they communicate online. As did that other large constituency she commanded, amongst the nation's youth.

EIGHT

On September 29th, she made the first announcement of the St Stephen's Day gathering. Had she relied on her own social media contacts it is unlikely that more than a couple of thousand would have answered the call. But due to the efforts of a veritable army of young people, who were entirely conversant with the internet and proficient in the dissemination of messages, it is estimated that upward of four million people had viewed her post by sunset that same evening.

Things, clearly, were out of hand. Not simply the continuing instances of suicides: but my mother had lost control of her message as well. She could neither halt the progress of the juggernaut she had helped to set in motion nor contribute further to legislative efforts to address the conditions which had brought about the 'terror'. She was side-lined, almost imprisoned, and unable as much as unwilling to accept this.

I think she knew the end was at hand. With hindsight, it was inevitable really. But neither she nor I knew exactly what would come to pass when we sat at the kitchen table each evening, our dinner set out on the old floral placemats with their scorched roses and saucepan marks, to talk over the minutia of the day. Which bulbs we would plant that year; the recent influx of new coffee shops on the main street (three such establishments having opened their doors in a three-month period); gossip about my ex-wife's romantic and social disasters (I appreciated my mother passing these on, regardless of the veracity of such tales) and her preferred choice of meal for the following days.

I had undertaken the role of cook during that time, surprised to discover that I was quite skilled in the kitchen and rather enjoyed the process of creating a meal. Her personal favourite, I remember, was cod cooked in white wine with slices of lemon, surrounded by spears of asparagus arranged in small bundles, which I wrapped in prosciutto. For breakfast she liked me to toast some brown soda bread, liberally cover it with tomato relish and top it with a soft poached egg and more asparagus tossed in butter. Her wee must have been quite green when she had these meals in close succession! But I am being boyish here, perhaps to stave off the memory of the less happy times which were to follow. I recall those meals together as blissful occasions and must confess to feeling somewhat grateful for her confinement during that short period, despite the difficulties it entailed for her.

She originally fixed upon October 31st for her gathering but I quickly dissuaded her, arguing that the advantages of it being a public holiday were outweighed by associations with the holiday itself. So it was that Friday October 21st was decided upon, despite my mother's misgivings about the length of time this would give her to mobilise an audience.

She need not have worried, as we know. But it is important to point out that she had neither the expectation nor indeed the desire to attract people in such numbers to the centre of the city, whatever accusation was subsequently levelled against her. Optimistically, she expected perhaps a couple of thousand, and it was with this figure in mind that we planned to hold the address at the fountains in the centre of St Stephen's Green. The record of the lengthy communication which passed between us (I assumed the role of event liaison) and the deputy police commissioner at Pearse Street Station will testify to this. It was always clear that they would grant our petition, given the level of public interest in both my mother herself, and the issues to be addressed at that gathering. An interest which became more emphatic once we revealed, in a series of confidential telephone calls with senior government officials - including, I can reveal, the Taoiseach himself - that my mother intended to use the occasion to call for a halt to the protests still riving the land.

This detail was not shared in any of the official and unofficial invites extended to what was effectively a global community. As we know, as many people travelled to (or back to) Ireland for that day as had flown in to register their support for the referendum on gay marriage. I suspect it was the very secrecy surrounding her motives for holding the gathering which fed interest in the event. The only thing people like more than a mystery is an enigma, and my mother had become one of recent weeks by virtue of her silence.

It is easy, with the supposed 'gift' of hindsight, to see why the final numbers wildly exceeded our expectations. Allied to the fact that this was a cause with a global following - and one which had dominated the news channels for several months - there was a collective desire to bring some sort of close to events. Things simmering for a lengthy period of time must, ultimately, come to the boil. What happened – and I fervently believe this – was as much the result of others' wishes as my mother's. As a species, we need resolution. And in matters of faith we invariably crucify our heroes.

I have always hated October. Eliot might have believed that April was the cruellest month, but what can be crueller or more likely to depress the spirits than the unequivocal end of summer, Indian or otherwise, and the inevitability of the cold, dark months ahead? That Friday was an exception to the norm of grey skies and rain, however, the sun throwing its spotlight on events throughout the day. Long sharp shadows crisscrossed the walkways about the green, set in continual motion as the wind stirred the trees at the edges of this verdant oasis. Huge seagulls bothered the ducks on the lake and screeched their displeasure at the poor pickings available after the death of summer. Bored guards walked up and down by the various entrances, wishing they were at some sporting event instead, half-heartedly scrutinising the contents of bags being carried into the Green by the early arrivals whose prescience in turning up ahead of time was proven once that first trickle turned into a flood, and word began to come in of a mass of people apparently making their way there, angry screeches coming now from shoulder-mounted walkie-talkies. It was not yet noon, and as word of the likely size of the attendance began to circulate, people began to turn up at an accelerated rate. By noon, there were over 20,000 people there, and my mother was not due to appear until three. One quick-thinking guard had the bright idea of borrowing some of the buskers from Grafton Street and throwing them in front of the crowd - for what would undoubtedly be the largest 'gig' they would ever do - as a means of keeping a restive crown entertained. As reinforcements began to arrive, and cordons were erected or moved to a more appropriate distance, four teenage students from Loreto On The Green played baroque pieces for string quartet and raised a sum beyond their wildest dreams for the St Vincent de Paul. Abandoning every city ordinance in favour of maintaining the prevailing calm, hotdog vendors and other purveyors of takeaway food were actively encouraged to enter the park and establish makeshift stalls catering to long lines of the politically active, but starving. The arrival of the first helicopter was greeted with cheers, and the realization that what they were involved in now was of significant import. And still the crowd swelled.

I was driving my mother along the Blackrock Road when a garda motorcycle appeared by the driver's window and instructed me to pull over. Her license plate was apparently known to them – which I should not have found surprising – and they had pulled us over to request that she avail of an escort into the Green in the hope that she would commence her address earlier than advertised, as a means of subduing the restless crowd. She refused, and was proved right at least in part when an estimated 50,000 more people were added to the numbers already assembled there between the hours of two and three. It might have been better, however, if she had heeded their advice.

The mood – despite the authorities' misgivings – was largely calm. Not exactly festive, but mannered and patient. Later estimates put the average age at 45, which is misleading as this is effectively a mean of the two dominant groups there, the over seventies and the under twenty-fives. Many touching unions of these groups were being enacted about the now crowded park, photos being taken and hats and other items of clothing exchanged, leading to some incongruous sights as pensioners sported beanies and tee-shirts instructing their peers to Obey, and teens worked their skilled way through the crowds in diamond-patterned woollen pullovers, doing that thing only kids of their age can do of making what they wore suddenly cool, rather than evident of a golf club membership.

And still they came, many abandoning any hope of gaining access to the park and wheedling their way into the buildings about all four sides of the park, which already sported hangers-out and observers in almost every window. Traffic diversions (for diversion read chaos) kept commuters away from the immediate area, and the Luas was forced to terminate at the Harcourt Street stop. Given that most of the Luas carriages were laden down with people drawn to the area from the well-heeled areas along the line it mattered little, as they were more than happy to walk down the hil,l and to take in the spectacle as they proceeded.

My mother's elderly Toyota Corolla was not the ideal vehicle in which to arrive at a rally. The helicopter shadowing her movements into the city no doubt hoped for something more distinctive, like a white jeep rather than a sliver saloon - one more anonymous family car with better than average mileage.

If my mother had already resolved upon her course of action, there was no sign of it. In truth, I believe she was in shock. Nothing could have prepared her for what she encountered as the traffic parted before us and we were escorted to the side entrance to the park opposite Dawson Street. No doubt it was deemed too dangerous or logistically difficult to bring her to the Soldier's Gate. We were shepherded from the car, which we left parked nose front behind the row of vehicles arranged along the South side opposite the Shelbourne Hotel, and were bustled in the narrow gateway and on through a throng of people which grew increasingly thick and loud as we approached the centre of the park. Word was spreading of her arrival, and what began as a rippled murmuration soon grew into the sort of fevered cheering which heralds the arrival of a rock act prior to their arrival on stage. In many ways, it was similar. The phalanx of security. The purposeful progress through those lucky enough to have secured a place close to the stage. The smiling, excited faces. All those hands reaching out between the policemen's arms to touch her, to form some sort of contact, however brief.

The greatest noise – the voices raised the highest – did not come from amongst the young, but the old. It was as if those so long denied a voice had found it magically restored, and all the frustrations they had bottled up had escaped the prison of silence in which they had been interned. It was extraordinary.

My skin still prickles at the memory of that vast outcry, spreading in waves from the centre as news of my mother's presence amongst them spread outward to those gathered at the very perimeter of the park and beyond. They were cheering themselves, of course. As does any large crowd. Congratulating each other for being there, and in such numbers. It seemed impossible that anyone would hear her speak once she reached the stage and ascended the podium, regardless of amplification. Like The Beatles at Shea Stadium!

The first sound as ever was a screech of feedback, which deafened those closest but served to quell the cacophony, a wave of quiet following the wave of noise as the vast crowd slowly fell silent.

There was no preamble, no introduction by an acolyte. Instead, a couple of Guards peeled off from the line surrounding the stage and led her directly to the tree of microphones arrayed at its centre. The insignia of a dozen TV and radio stations could be seen on the bulblike protrudences.

Those expecting my mother to tremble before the spectacle which greeted her on gaining the podium did not know her. She had always reacted to a crisis with unruffled sufficiency. When things grew hectic, she grew calm. I can recall her attending the victim of a traffic accident on the main street of Blackrock. A young mother and her child of two or three had been thrown across the bonnet of a Ford Fiesta to land in the centre of the road, blood pooling about the mother's head while she groaned and reached an exhausted hand toward her daughter, who lay equally flat and silent, wrapped in a quilted jacket the ambulance crew who attended them later posited had likely saved her from serious injury, or worse. While others held their hands before their faces aghast, or bustled about ineffectively waiting for somebody else to summon the emergency services, my mother strode out before the offending car and knelt by the mother, having quickly established that the child was essentially unharmed, one hand holding her mobile phone to her mouth and the other sweeping the hair back from the young woman's forehead to ascertain the extent of her injuries. She was ever thus; and that sense of quiet purpose was again in evidence in a circumstance which would have overwhelmed nine-hundred-and-ninety-five out of a thousand. She was indomitable. Fearless. Fixed of purpose and unwavering. I do not believe I had ever been as proud of her as I was at that moment, watching her stand patiently by the microphones while she waited for silence.

"Will they ignore us now?" she asked, having forced them through sheer power of will to quell their noise. This question brought forth a huge cheer, vastly exceeding the excited exhortations directed toward the stage, before she commenced her address. It took a full minute before the noise was hushed, and she was able to continue.

"Will they disregard us? Will they dismiss us, or insult us with their empty platitudes and ineffective decrees? We are stronger than that. Stronger than them!"

Another huge cheer.

"You have done a remarkable thing. You, not I. Take this moment to celebrate your own power, your own commitment to bettering the lives of those so long discriminated against. For you are mighty, and your voice will *not* be ignored! You no longer have to lay suit to them to change their ways, or beg them to do that which they must. You are now their masters! They are the servants to your will. What they would not do — what they refused to do in their arrogance and ignorance - they must do now. Demand it! Make the sacrifices of all those who have fallen for this cause meaningful, and rip justice from the arms of those who denied it to them! If you see any law which treats those of advanced years as the lesser - smash it down!"

An enormous roar. "Cast it down and ground it into sand. Leave nothing standing which would hold you back!"

The rest you know. It is one of the most quoted speech of our generation, although I myself still find it somewhat grandiose, and less eloquent that her earlier, more direct avowals. Not flowery as such, or verbose… but a thing of artifice rather than passion I feel. A fine speech no doubt, but less true of her than her outburst on the Dan Crowley Show, or the plain talk of her many interviews. Much as I admire it, I do not hold it in the respect it has been accorded of recent times. My mother was a better agitator than a demagogue, I would vouchsafe. Perhaps only Christ himself could master both.

Who first lit the spark which transformed the crowd from a peaceful gathering to a rabid horde has never been established. Perhaps it was, as many commentators have suggested, an example of the phenomenon we call mass hysteria. Perhaps - as others have conjectured - there was a deliberate attempt to sabotage the event, and to subvert the message my mother wished to deliver. Whatever the cause, the result was the same. I spent months reviewing the news footage and the desperate images captured with mobile phones and posted on YouTube and

Facebook. Perhaps I thought I would see something invisible to all the others who have done the same. I don't know. Or perhaps I thought my claim upon her would lend me knowledge denied them and allow me to solve the mystery, so that I would not have to close my account with yet more speculation. But it was not to be. I will restrict myself, therefore, to the facts as they have been established, and add the details of what we ourselves experienced around the podium and in its aftermath. I suspect much of this shall be new to you – and may well contradict the received wisdom, established as that might be. For my mother's 'sacrifice' was not as it appears.

NINE

Depending on which estimate you accept, there were between 150,000 and 250,000 people in the environs of St Stephen's Green Dublin when the chaos began. It started – this much is uncontested – in two separate areas of the park. By the same entrance opposite Dawson Street where my mother and I had entered, and almost directly across from there by the pathway on the North side, opposite the headquarters of the Football Association of Ireland.

This was the largest public gathering to take place on Irish soil since the visit of Pope John Paul II in 1979. But whereas that event had been meticulously planned, with wide thoroughfares carved out between each corral of spectators - Phoenix Park being a vast area, well capable of accommodating what is believed to have been over a million people – the crowd which assembled in St Stephen's Green was many times greater than had been forecast, and the environs were quite unsuited to such a press of people. Strange as it might sound, there are few open spaces in the park.

The perimeters consist of pathways with mature growth, large trees and other planting, encroaching upon what in many places is quite a narrow passage, capable of accommodating no more than three abreast. The lake at the Southern end takes up approximately 15% of the entire space and the undulating nature of the landscaping, allied to the presence of so many trees and bushes, meant that there were few spaces outside of the central area by the fountains which offered a direct line of sight to the podium where my mother stood. The amplification, hastily erected, was also incapable of reaching many areas of the park, meaning that for most the speeches were relayed on mobile phones or car radios, knots of people gathering about these points, creating small satellites and no small amount of frustration. There was fear, too. Those who had arrived early and brought children with them now found themselves trapped in the very centre of the park with no path to an exit, and the distress of some of these children was evident even before the panic started. Those at the front could not get out, and those at the back were relentless in their efforts to edge closer, or to force their way between the bodies in front of them to gain a vantage point from which to see and hear proceedings. The guards – to their credit – did manage to clear three narrow pathways with the help of further reinforcements. But few of those gathered had access to these routes or could even spy them through the throng.

In truth, the authorities were in an impossible situation. Any attempt to interrupt proceedings – even to use bullhorns to encourage sections of the crowd to move away from the pathways – would have been interpreted as an attempt to silence my mother, and could have resulted in a hostile response. So too would any effort to turn people away, or to force them to quit the Green. In the event, there were many who ascribed the panic which followed to actions taken by the police, as ill-informed as this was. Rumours of police heavy-handedness however added to the chaos.

It needs to be placed on record that there is no fair comparison between the actions of the Irish Garda and those of the police at Hillsborough Stadium in 1989. There, impatience and a lack of concern for the safety of football fans decisively contributed to the deaths of the 96 people who lost their lives. In many ways, of course, there were similarities. A crush of people attempting to gain access to an area ringed about with iron railings. A heightened atmosphere, part expectation, part euphoria. A complete failure of the chain of command, though in this instance because there were simply too few personnel and too many immediate situations to be dealt with to occupy the individual officers who did so much that day to minimise the loss of life, and to provide assistance to those who required it. Far from being the agents of a repressive regime, the Guards - to a man and women - acted in the best interests of the people, in what were nigh-impossible conditions.

And in the end, it took so little. If the crush of bodies was the kindling and my mother's oration served to raise the temperature, then all it needed was one spark to ignite the lot.

For whatever reason – a stumble which rippled outward and grew into a crush, or through the deliberate or selfish efforts of some small number trying to force their way through those standing before them, a surge occurred on the Southern side of the park which was echoed almost immediately on the opposite side. At first, it appeared the wave would break, as people took refuge in the still unoccupied areas filled with planting, creating a space for the force to dissipate. But others took advantage of the spaces opened up by their absence and drove the crush onward until it met a solid wall of bodies with nowhere to go but inward... or down.

Those first screams of terror are still chilling to hear. To begin with, the reaction from those closest to the podium was muted, with some mutterings about the police potentially seeking to halt proceedings... but no inkling of what was to befall them. It took less than a minute however for those outer waves to roll inward, and for the full horror to unfold.

In such circumstances, it is said, the most important thing to do is to stay on your feet. Even if you find yourself being lifted upward or carried forward, the essential thing is to remain upright, for once you fall beneath such an enormous crush it is virtually impossible to regain your feet, and your chances of surviving the onslaught of feet and knees about your head, combined with a lack of oxygen which can quickly render you unconscious, lessen by the second. As difficult as this might sound, it is better for a parent to release their grip upon their offspring and allow them to be carried away from them than to try to drag them toward themselves against the crush. Better, but instinctively impossible. What mother or father would choose to let go of their child's hand in such circumstances? And what of those whose children were inside buggies, or perched aloft upon their fathers' shoulders?

In the event, there were soon two waves seething through the throng: the first moving inexorably toward the centre from those two outward swells; and a second circulating about the perimeter of the park, as those closest to an exit desperately sought to leave. Though in time this second wave would free up space and provide relief for those gathered closer in, the first effect of this was to drive people against the railings, there being so few and such narrow gates offering egress from the Green. And as the panic grew, and the desperation of those trying to find a way out increased, the crush of people relentlessly shifted towards those ornate but unyielding barriers. The railings surrounding St Stephen's Green are high and topped with spikes. Though largely decorative, they do have the purpose of discouraging anyone from climbing into the park after closing hours, and form a relatively effective deterrent. As a result, however, they placed those trapped inside in an impossible situation. Too high to climb, too dangerous to scale - and utterly unyielding to the pressure of those forced up against them.

There were myriad examples of heroism that day along the four sides of the park. The doormen from the Merrion Hotel who ran several hundred yards carrying the Persian rug from the entrance lobby and draped it across the spikes on the Northwest corner, balancing on the outside of the railings to heave body after body up and over the railing to safety. The clamping crew who used the tensile winch normally used to remove illegally parked vehicles to wrench a twelve-foot length of railing from the Eastern side of the Green opposite Ely Place, an action which doubtless saved lives and did much to alter long-held perceptions of the character of those in such employ. The motorists and cab drivers who forced their way onto the outer pathway to park their vans, 4x4's and people carriers parallel to the railings, standing atop them and using their roofs to create vital bridges to escape. The window cleaners who converted their ladders into scaffolds. All of these actions – and the vital role that the trees around the hedges played in offering a fire-break for the crush – allowed the majority of those seeking escape to exit the park with minimal damage to life and limb. Barely ten minutes after the first surge Harcourt Street, Lesson Street, Dawson and Kildare Streets and Merrion Row were full of distraught, but largely unharmed people, clinging to each other in shock and distress as the realisation hit of how close they had come to an horrendous death, many still in a state of panic as they sought to locate friends and relatives from whom they had become separated.

That no one else died that day is a miracle. Before the first wave crested in the centre of the park, however, more than fifty people would lose the battle to remain upright and to resist the pressure of the tens of thousands of bodies pressing upon them, some suffering serious injury in the process. Four of these – Janet Egan aged four, Melanie Costello and Niamh Neary, both aged twelve and Cian Murphy, just two and a half years old – were children. I often wonder how my mother would have reacted to news of their injuries, or if some of these had died. Would she have despaired? Or had she already resolved to bring an end to the movement which she had, if not led, then at least championed?

What nobody expected, as the crush rushed relentlessly inward toward the rickety stage, was for her to pull out a gun from her purse. I can excuse my own inertia at that moment by explaining that this was no ordinary gun, but one I instinctively knew to be the one my father had used to take his own life. My very heart stopped at the sight, and I found myself immobilised with fright at the thought of what might follow.

There are conflicting views as to whether firing a gun above the heads of an onrushing crowd is more likely to halt or to accelerate the rush of bodies in a situation of this nature. Some have even suggested that it was blind panic and self-interest which led my mother to fire the weapon. This is errant nonsense. At no stage had the panic about her affected her own demeanour and – whatever the reason she had transported it there that day (through successive police escorts!) – she utilised it in a deliberate manner, even ensuring that the gun was discharged directly beside a microphone in order to amplify the sound. The effect was instantaneous. With that sharp retort, which echoed about the buildings on all four sides of the Green, the impetus for the crush toward the stage was immediately removed, with people literally rocked back upon their heels. Fearing that her discharging of the weapon would give the authorities an immediate cause to detain her – despite the clear good which resulted – a phalanx drawn from amongst the organisers quickly drew about us both, and shepherded us away from the stage.

TEN

My mother had feet of clay. She had no intention of dying that day, let alone at her own hand. She had brought the gun, I believe, because in recent days she had received a flurry of death threats. These were nothing new in themselves; but these latest ones were quite specific, and included details of her home and habits which suggested the threat was both close at hand, and real.

She was, at the very least, a reluctant martyr, as distressing as this might be to those who have sought to idolize her. As I have often stated, she was neither the devil nor the angel she has been painted as. Apart from anything else, she had long regarded suicide as a coward's way out - hence the fact that in all those years we had never spoken of nor acknowledged the nature of my father's death. I was in my late twenties before I learned of it. A friendly doctor of our faith had conspired with my mother to keep the true cause of his death a secret, to ensure that my mother was not deprived of his life insurance. Together, they had calmly placed his body on a chair in his beloved potting shed and doused him with fuel from the lawnmower, before setting the shed alight to disguise all traces of the true cause of his demise. When the police arrived the doctor was on hand to determine the cause of death as a massive heart attack whilst he had been filling the mower with his pipe between his teeth. The bullet had exited his skull, and the doctor later disposed of it in the sea near to his surgery. How ironic that her rise to prominence would come on the back of so many other suicides, and that her own life would end in such a way!

The environs of St Stephen's Green were in turmoil. First the crush, and the panic which ensued - and then gunfire, its source unclear. Those who had managed to escape the park rushed away down the surrounding streets. Grafton Street, Dawson Street, Kildare Street, Ely Place, Lesson Street, Harcourt Street: Prouds Lane and York Street, Glovers Alley and Kings Street South past the Gaiety Theatre as far as Chatham Street filled with people, driving each other onwards in a contagion of panic, people afraid to turn around until they had found some place of safety. The narrow exits to the park however ensured that there were still several thousand who believed themselves trapped in the presence of a gunman, so the turmoil inside the park was heightened by much screaming and wailing, all of which provided a cover of sorts for my mother's makeshift honour guard as they marshalled us toward the Merrion Row end. She had returned the gun to her handbag as we fled, avoiding an attempt by one of those escorting her to take possession of it, presumably with the intention of discarding it.

Garda reinforcements had been summoned, but their numbers were already so stretched that a decision was made to mobilise the Special Branch and the anti-terrorist division, once reports had confirmed that a gun had been fired. As a result, armed men could be seen entering the park through several of the entrances, many of them in plain clothes. None of the authorities at this point seemed aware of the fact that it had been my mother who had loosed the shot, the camera crews' attention having been fixed upon the surge of people approaching the stage from the opposite direction, and at least one TV crew having abandoned their duties – and their equipment - in the name of self-preservation.

At the north-eastern edge of the Green there is a memorial to the Great Famine by the sculptor Edward Delaney. It depicts two standing figures, one with arms uplifted and the other feeding a seated figure with a ladle, while a hound lies nearby. To the rear of the statues is a row of stone pillars roughly twenty feet in height, arranged in a semi-circle with their edges curving away from these figures toward the park. It was to the rear of these, sheltered within that stone bay, that my mother and I and a swollen cohort of her supporters came to a stop. In all, I estimate that there were between twenty to thirty of us, my mother concealed in the centre of the knot of bodies. To pass beyond this point would mean leaving the park for the road outside, where the police presence was heavy and she might easily be spotted. Most people ignored us, streaming past on either side of the pillars in order to escape. A calm descended. We were safe now, we knew, the crush having dissipated, and we might well have smuggled her out at this point had anyone thought to do so. But she seemed paralysed by the scene, staring at this flood of distressed people like a sleepwalker suddenly awoken. Did I cause this, her expression seemed to ask? It seemed impossible that no one had died, and I suspect the likelihood of such an outcome had already dawned upon her. And those most likely to have perished were the elderly, and the young. Children, and those she had sought to protect! Her whole face appeared to cave. I remember fighting past a few of those ranked about her, feeling concern and – yes – pity for her at that moment. I have no doubt the weight of those thoughts sat heavy upon her and her conscience. She was not to know – irony of ironies – that her own actions had prevented the loss of many lives, or that no one had in fact perished in the surge of bodies she had witnessed from her perch upon the stage. No: in her mind people had died, and she was at least in part responsible. What must have been going through her mind? Regret, that she had not sought to postpone the event once the numbers became unmanageable? The suspicion that her own pride might have prevented such a course of action? Shame? Despair? We will never know. All I know, I know from reading her face – I, who had watched that face and learned how to read those expressions from the very cradle.

"Mother!" I shouted, though I was but a foot from her side. The noise of sirens and car horns and the yelling of those about us was deafening.

My cry seemed to pull her from her trance. She smiled at me, and called my name! There were other words, but it took me a further minute or two to get close enough to hear her.

"It's all right," I said, attempting to reassure her, placing an arm about her shoulder as much to assert my right to primacy as to shelter her. I was shaking, I remember. From adrenalin, if you are being kindly. But from fear also. Those past minutes, whilst we scurried ahead of a press of bodies threatening to upend and trample us at any moment, were terrifying. I was hyperventilating, unable to catch my breath. I was soaked with sweat, my mouth so dry that my words escaped me in a sort of hoarse growl. My mother, however, had regained her composure, watching the flood of bodies pass as if she were remote from it – as if she were viewing television footage of the event from our sitting room at some later time, far from the danger and the noise.

"No, Dominic. It is not okay."

We stayed there, huddled in the shelter of those rocks, for roughly twenty minutes, waiting for the tumult to abate and for things about us to settle. Police were entering the park in numbers at this point, escorting medical staff, seeking out the injured and the lost, some pushing gurneys unloaded from the ambulances now pulling to a halt without. The lights of the emergency vehicles flashed blue and red in the gaps between the pillars, painting the backs and shoulders of those huddled about us. I was reminded of the aftermath of Rose Connolly's self-sacrifice, outside the gates of Leinster House. Looking back, however, I cannot be sure that I did not conjure up this comparison at some later date in an attempt to fashion a neat coda to events. My mother watched, detached and silent. And then she stood up and shot herself.

ELEVEN

The following few weeks were a blur, and I'm afraid there is little I can share with you about that time. That time after I watched my mother blow her brains out, to bring a halt to it all.

I am certain that this was her intent. Just as her first shot had sought to stop the crush before the stage, this second one was intended to end the carnival of death which preceded it. Which is why I told the press what I did. You can condemn me for lying about my mother's final words, but I feel they were accurate in their sentiment, and subsequent events have vindicated me. Perhaps she had said as much as I fought my way through to her? "This has to end." Not bad, really, for one unaccustomed to lying. It was what she thought, I know; if not what she said. My conscience is clear.

And where did all this leave me, then? Alone.

I am on my own now, of course. An orphan - as ridiculous a term as this is to assign to a man in his middle-age. In ways though I had always been so. Why else would I have been so pathetically grateful for the time she spent with me in those last months? Treating me like a servant, and only conversing with me because of the lack of an alternate? Goodness – not just an orphan! An orphan loses both its parents, together or singularly. My parents thought so little of me that they both killed themselves to escape me. And what does that say about their only son?

I can grant them their good intentions. My father's wish to save his family from the knowledge of his ruin; my mother's wish to halt the carnage her 'movement' had incited. It did not work, of course. At least not immediately. There were further suicides both abroad and at home – particularly when it seemed that the government of the day were seeking to exploit her absence to renege on some of their promises – but gradually these changed from a flood to a trickle, as new laws and improved oversight for the aged lessened, if not removed, the grievances which had fuelled the protests.

What did not change – and still exists today – is our fear of the elderly. I myself am not ageist (how could I be!) but still find it difficult not to view them as something 'other'. They steal about amongst us, revelling in their power over us. Every institution favours them, their power focused now on the political process, where they continue to vote en-masse and in concert, allowing them to exert what some would say is a disproportionate influence upon politicians and lawmakers. They make their way about our streets, heads held high despite their shrunken stature, often forming bands and causing those before them to step out of their path. They slow the traffic on our roads (maliciously, in many cases) and seem to delight in making others wait at cash registers and post office counters. Their command of social media puts teenagers to shame; apparently able to mobilise in moments, in response to any perceived slight and maintaining a constant communication with their peers which stretches across social and geographic boundaries. I admire them, as we must. But – and I dare say we all think this, even if the sentiment is seldom spoken aloud – I fear them also. As Dan Crowley said, under my mother's watch their target was themselves.

Next time, it will be us.

Also by Steven Duggan

The Loss of Ordinary Plenty
The Dead Dane
Virgins

To contact the author email
stevenduggan@hotmail.com

Steven is represented by Phil Patterson at
Marjacq Scripts
R24 Offices
103 Kingsway
London WC2B 6QX
www.Marjacq.com

Printed in Great
Britain
by Amazon